Merry Christmas!

The Santa Train
and other stories of the season

[signature]

JERRY PETERSON

This book is a work of fiction. Names, characters, places and incidents are the products of the author's imagination or are used fictitiously. All characters in this book have no existence outside the imagination of the author and have no relationship to anyone, living or dead, bearing the same name or names. All incidents are pure invention from the author's imagination. Any resemblance to actual events or locales or persons, living or dead, is entirely coincidental.

All Rights Reserved. Except for use in any review, the reproduction or utilization of this work in whole or in part in any form by any electronic, mechanical or other means, now known or hereafter invented, including xerography, photocopying or recording, or in any information or retrieval system, is forbidden without the prior written permission of both the publisher and copyright owner of this book.

Copyright 2013 c Jerry Peterson
Grand Jubilee Books

All Rights Reserved.

ISBN-13: 978-1492771326
ISBN-10: 1492771325

Cover Design c Dawn Charles at
bookgraphics.wordpress.com

October 2013

Printed in the U.S.A.

Dedication

To Marge, my wife and first reader.

To the members of my writers group – *Tuesdays with Story* – sharp-eyed readers and writers who demand the very best of me in my storytelling and writing.

To a friend and one-time colleague who prefers to remain unnamed.

And to all people who love Christmas. That includes you, dear reader.

Acknowledgments

This is the sixth book I've published as indie author, the second under my Grand Jubilee Books imprint.

Most writers work alone. Still, those of us who do, we depend on others to make our stories and our books the best that they can be. For me, those 'others' include the members of my writers group – Tuesdays with Story – and Dawn Charles of Book Graphics, cover designer extraordinaire. Dawn worked my cover project in between a cover she was designing for a French writer and formatting her own cookbook, so I could get *Santa Train* out on schedule. Dawn does sterling work.

I always close with a note of appreciation to all librarians around the country. They, like you and your fellow readers who have enjoyed my James Early mysteries and my AJ Garrison crime novels have been real boosters.

Without them and you, there would be no reason to write.

A note from the author

One of the first questions readers ask at book talks is, where do your ideas come from?

For "Santa Train", some several years ago when I was a graduate student at the University of Tennessee, I read a story about the real Santa train that for 69 years now has made an annual run through the Appalachians, from Pikeville, Kentucky, to Kingsport, Tennessee, taking Christmas to families who have known hard times in the coalfields.

I liked the idea of the Santa train. For my story, I took it back in time to 1936 and placed my train in the Smoky Mountains, taking Christmas to families devastated by the end of the timber industry in the mountains.

I needed a Santa and found him in a circuit-riding preacher, John Hepsebah Lawless. You're going to like him.

"Holly and Mistletoe" originally saw life as a chapter in *The Watch*, my first AJ Garrison crime novel. My writers group forced me to kill the chapter in the second draft of the manuscript because, as several members said, the Christmas story had nothing to do with the crime Garrison was investigating. "The Sister Trees", as I had titled the chapter, was a distraction.

They were correct.

Well, writers never throw anything away. I liked that chapter, so I rewrote it into a short story that could stand up all by itself, a story of how a young couple in love, a couple who have very little money for Christmas, make due with a pair of misshapen Christmas trees a tree seller had intended to chop up for firewood.

"Bump and the Stranger" is the final story in this Christmas trio. I read a stripped down version of it somewhere along the line and knew there was more in there than the original author saw.

My character, Bump Asher, is a gas station owner and mechanic who finds it hard to keep Christmas because he's alone. His wife has died and he has no children. On the afternoon of Christmas Eve, just as he's about to close the station, the Stranger walks in, a young guy wearing a jacket from Vietnam war . . . and the war's been over for 20 years.

You're going to be surprised who the guy is.

Also by Jerry Peterson

James Early Mysteries
    Book 1, *Early's Fall*
    Book 2, *Early's Winter*

AJ Garrison Crime Novels
    Book 1, *The Watch*
    Book 2, *Rage*

Wings Over the Mountains Novels
    Book 1, *The Last Good Man*

Short story collections
    A James Early Christmas & Other Stories of the Season

The Santa Train

Word came to the preacher—Preacher John Hepsebah Lawless—that a message waited for him at the bishop's office.

"Know what it's about?" he asked a fellow circuit rider who, unlike him, worked the lowland churches out of Pigeon Forge.

"Nary an idee. Might you be in some trouble, John?"

"Lordy, no. Least I don't think so. Still I'd better get up there and beard the old lion."

Lawless pushed Sandy, the Belgian work horse that carried the beefy man from one home church to the next in the high back country of the Smoky Mountains, through three-foot deep snowdrifts to Sevierville.

At Wilson's Livery, he led the exhausted animal into a stall, the building warm from the body heat of a dozen other horses. There was the sweet smell of clover hay. Lawless liked that. He forked a bunch into the feed bunk for Sandy before he toweled her dry.

From the livery, Lawless hoofed it to the East Tennessee, Virginia & Georgia depot, intent on catching the Number Eleven to Knoxville. An intercity bus service connected the foothills country town to the university city, but most people skipped it in the winter for the never-fail Mountain Hummer, as the ETV&G was known.

Lawless wasn't much for riding in the Hummer's passenger cars. The seats were too small for someone who tipped the scale outside the local drugstore at two hundred forty pounds. Lawless could wedge himself in. When he had to, he took an aisle seat so he had somewhere to park his legs. Then people had to step over him, so he preferred to ride in the caboose where he could sprawl out on a bench seat and pass the time with the conductor. And there was coffee, lots of it from the pot the conductor kept on the caboose's stove. On this short run, Lawless had the end car and the coffee to himself. The conductor stayed forward in the passenger cars.

The hot brew warmed Lawless's innards. That and the heat from the stove soon placed him in the arms of Morpheus. There Lawless snoozed until a jostling woke him, the Number Eleven rocking through several switches on its way into the Southern rail yard at Knoxville. He roused himself, shook out the kinks, gathered his gear, and took to shank's mare for the ten blocks to the bishop's office on Commerce Street.

A tiny woman–tiny compared to Lawless's mass– answered his knock. She fascinated him every time he came, so bird-like, with the energy of a house wren, forever flitting about the bishop's offices, twittering on without end.

She smiled up at Lawless, chirping, "Come in, come in, but do be careful not to shake snow all over. Mister Lawless, isn't it wonderful, this snow we have, just perfect for an old-fashioned Christmas, wouldn't you say? The bishop's expecting you, he's been expecting you for two weeks now, wherever have you been? You didn't fall in with some Cherokee woman up there in the wilds, did you? The both of us were worried so, when we hadn't heard from you. You know, Mister

Lawless, you really ought to get a telephone—they're calling it an Ameche now—or the least you could do is write to us once in a while. What is going on up there in the mountains? Have you started any new churches we should put on our list, deacons we should be mailing things to?"

Lawless knew better than to interrupt. He set his saddlebags and bedroll in a corner by the street door where he could retrieve them quickly if he had to make a hurried escape. Then he pulled off his mackinaw and caulk boots. He tossed them in the corner as well, and his striped railroad cap that someone had given him. Next he shook the snow out of the fringes of his hair and his great red beard, creating a small blizzard in the front hallway.

"Are you ever going to get a haircut, Mister Lawless?" the little woman went on. "For as long as the bishop and I have known you, you have looked like the wild man of Borneo. And that beard, really. Methodist ministers just don't have beards anymore. Beards went out with the tintypes and button shoes. Now you just wait here, and I'll tell the bishop. And please be careful of the carpeting—your pant legs are dripping."

Lawless glanced down.

Miss Angelica Smith flitted away, down the hall to a side office. "I just don't understand what it is about Mister Lawless," she said to the person inside, "but he never says anything. Leaves it all to me to carry both sides of the conversation."

"I do share your concern," came an answering voice, a man's voice. Lawless recognized it—the bishop, Walter Atherton. "Miss Angelica, please, if you would be so kind, send that raggedy old man in here. I'll see if I can pry three words out of him. And would you get us a coffee?"

Miss Angelica Smith flitted back up the hallway. "The bishop will see you," she said and fluttered on to her own office.

Lawless, in his stockinged feet, shlepted his way down the hall, wondering whether he was about to have his ears blistered. He tapped on the doorjamb.

Atherton, at his desk, laid his spectacles aside. He massaged the bridge of his nose. "Little John, how are you?" he asked.

"Am I in trouble, bish?"

"Could be." Atherton pulled open a side drawer. He brought out three envelopes, each a pastel blue. "John, what are you doing, getting letters from a married woman? And an Episcopalian?"

Lawless's brow furrowed.

"Well, speak up, man."

Atherton held out the envelopes.

Lawless took them. He peered at the back of one, then the next, and the third. *Mrs. A.G. King . . . Mrs. A.G. King . . . Mrs. A.G. King . . .*

He turned the last one over. It was addressed to him, care of the bishop's office, he saw it, and in the lower right corner, a single word–'Urgent.'

Atherton, his triple chins suggesting he had missed few church dinners, settled back in his leather chair. "I know who she is, John. Her husband's a lumber baron up there in those mountains of yours. He owns a railroad. I almost opened the letters."

Lawless tore the end off the envelope. He blew into it and, with two fingers, extracted the enclosure. He read it. "Bishop, it says here she's got something for me at the rail yard. No mention of what it is, just that I got to get it to Townsend before the Twenty-Fourth."

Lawless stuffed the letter in his pocket. He took a seat on the bishop's side chair, and it creaked beneath his weight. There Lawless opened the second envelope. As he read, his mouth gaped.

"John, is there a problem?"

Miss Angelica Smith bustled in with a silver tray on which rode not cups of coffee, but two steaming mugs of mulled cider. "Joy of the season," she said to Lawless as she set one of the mugs on the desk beside him. She held the tray out to the bishop. "Joy of the season."

"Joy of the season to you, Miss Angelica." The bishop inhaled the aroma rising from his mug of cider. "It is a joy, and you, Miss Angelica, are a blessing."

She beamed.

"Oh yes, thank you," Lawless mumbled while he folded his letter.

"Well, I see you got four words out of him," the house wren said. She backed out of the office and closed the door.

Atherton drummed his fingers on his desk as he peered at his circuit rider. "Your letter, John?"

Lawless let out a low whistle. "As some of the men in my mountain congregations would say, it's the damnedest thing."

The bishop choked. He spit a mouthful of cider back in his mug.

"Bishop, I'm sorry. Let me start over." Lawless held the letter between his index fingers. He leaned toward Atherton. "It's a miracle. Missus King says her husband's going to give us everything we need to build a hospital."

The bishop choked a second time.

"Your drink a bit hot, bish?"

Atherton dabbed a handkerchief at the driblets of cider on his chins. "No, no, it's just that—John, what hospital?"

"There's so much sickness back there deep in the mountains. Missus King was traveling with me, and she saw some of it. I told her what we needed was a hospital. Actually, Doc Schroeder called it a sanatorium because our biggest problem right now is consumption."

"Just a minute. Back up here just a minute. Have I got this right, John? You were traveling around in those mountains of yours with this married woman?"

"Yessir."

"Was her husband with her? With, you know, with the both of you?"

"No sir. Mister King doesn't get out of Townsend much, except to go up to Pittsburgh on business."

Atherton set his mug down, his hand trembling. "So now—you—uhmm, ahh—you, a man of the cloth, you were alone with this married woman, traveling together?"

"Yessir, some of the time."

"John, I'm not sure I want to hear the rest of this unless we were to adjourn and go down the street to Saint Mary's, and you were to agree to go in for confession."

"Bishop, what are you talking about?"

"You and this married woman traveling together."

"But Doc Schroeder was with us. Well, most of the time, anyway."

"And his wife, she was there, too?"

"Oh no, she lives in Maryville. Never goes up in the mountains."

"John—"

Lawless straightened up. "Wait a minute, you think there's something—"

"What else can I think?"

"Look, bish, this woman's got money. I figured she might help some of the families her husband had thrown out of work if she could see them. She agreed to if I'd guide her to Rainbow Falls."

"But you said a hospital. What's a hospital got to do with helping people out of work?"

"It's caring for the sick. People out of work, bishop, they'd rather help themselves. They don't want charity."

"This sure sounds like charity to me."

Lawless slapped the letter on the desk. "Good gosh, bishop, our congregation at Fish Camp is going to build it themselves. And the lumber and all, well, maybe that's just justice. After all, most of these people worked for the lumber companies 'til the companies quit cuttin' in their areas. Maybe this is—well, call it delayed pay."

Lawless ripped the end off the third envelope. A small note fluttered to the floor as he pulled out a letter. Lawless opened it. He let his gaze play down the page.

"Hallelujah!" Lawless jumped up and shook the letter in the bishop's face. "Look at this! Just look at this!"

Atherton made a grab for the paper.

"Missus King got the money! One of her friends in Philadelphia says she'll put up the money to run the hospital. Bishop, this thing isn't going to cost anybody up there a Lincoln-head penny."

"Or us?"

Lawless paced, his mind in overdrive. "Bishop, God told me this was never to be a district thing. This is His people's project. This is Jesus's people doing for themselves, maybe with a little help from an interested soul here and there, but it's them doing for themselves."

The bishop's secretary bustled in. She plucked up the note from the floor. "Mister Lawless, I don't appreciate you littering our offices. You may live in a pig sty up there, but down here in Knoxville we don't."

She slapped the note in his hand and stalked out.

Lawless leaned out the door to apologize, but the house wren had already flown from sight. He gazed at the note, lined paper torn from a child's writing tablet. Lawless recognized the pencil scrawl. He collapsed on the side chair where he wadded the paper into a ball.

Atherton stared at him.

Lawless threw the balled-up page in the bishop's wastebasket. "The park won't give us the land." He stared out the window, a man lost, empty, as if his heart had been torn from him.

Atherton retrieved the note. He smoothed it on his desk before he pulled his spectacles over and hooked the bows over his ears.

"Who's this Boggs Kuhfuss?" he asked when he got to the bottom of the lined page.

"My deacon at Fish Camp. He must have sent the note to Missus King, and she put it in with her letter without reading it."

"And a Mister Hansen?"

"Per Hansen, the park's assistant warden. Bish, we wanted to lease some land for the hospital. Hansen said he'd take it to the superintendent. You read it. Boggs says we got turned down—all our work, all our prayers, why'd we ever bother?"

Atherton fixed his gaze on his circuit rider. "Superintendent? The park superintendent?"

"Yeah."

"John, that's Henry Wentworth. Don't you know him?"

Lawless slumped on his chair.

"He's on the board at our Sevierville church. Of course, you don't know him. You never visit that church." Atherton pushed away from his desk. He leaned out into the hallway. "Miss Angelica?"

"Yes, bishop?"

"Would you get Henry Wentworth on the telephone? He's at the national park office in Gatlinburg. Tell whoever answers that God's calling."

"What are you doing?" Lawless asked.

Atherton shushed him with a wave of his hand.

Small footsteps hurried down the hall, and then the house wren stood perched in the doorway of the bishop's office, looking most pleased with herself. "Mister Wentworth is on the Ameche."

"Miss Angelica, you are a miracle worker." Atherton swept the receiver up from his desk telephone and pressed it to his ear. "Henry? . . . No, this isn't God," he said, chuckling. "This is the bishop . . . How's the wife, Henry?"

Atherton sat down on his leather chair. He leaned back, a hand cupped behind his head. "And the children? . . . Got any snow down there? . . . That's nice. We've got some up here, makes the city look like a Christmas card. Henry, why I'm calling, my minister of missions is here in my office. He works up in your park. . . . Yes, we've got a church up there at Fish Camp, and my minister of missions tells me you turned down their request for land for a hospital . . . You didn't know this was a Methodist thing? Well, your man must have forgotten to tell you . . . Uh-huh, yes, it does have the district's blessing . . . You say you still can't authorize a lease for that land? . . . Well, what's it going to take, Henry? . . . You'd have to buck it to Washington? . . . Henry, those people are up to their eyebrows, fighting this depression. They're not going to take kindly to being bothered with a small-potatoes thing like this. How do you think this is going to look on your record? . . . That's not important to you?"

Atherton came forward, fire in his eyes. He planted his elbows on his desk. "Well, Henry, let me ask you, how do you like your job? . . . You like it just fine? I'm glad to hear that because I know the people who got you appointed to that job, and three of them are devout, upstanding Methodists. Now, Henry, I don't want you to take this as a threat, but a couple telephone calls and you won't have a job. . . . You say you think you could see your way clear to giving this a second think? . . . Well, that's mighty Christian of you. Tell me, Henry, when could you give it a second think? . . . Right now? . . . Excellent. Excellent decision. Henry, would you do the paperwork on that lease today and get it on up to our Fish Camp congregation? It'd make a mighty nice Christmas present for them, don't you think? . . . Yes, yes, God's speed. I'm praying for you . . . Yes, and you have a good Christmas, too."

Atherton placed the receiver back on the telephone's cradle, a smile tugging at the corners of his mouth.

Miss Angelica Smith gazed at the bishop, radiant. "It appears you are the miracle worker."

He gave a modest wave. "How about you refill our mugs?" he said.

She collected the tray and mugs and disappeared.

Atherton, twirling his spectacles by one of their bows, looked at Lawless. "Is it going to be a good Christmas, John?"

****

The Knoxville station agent—Charles Rumford—and Lawless rambled out to the platform, "The Old Man must think you're pretty important," Rumford said, "for him to send his personal railroad car for you."

"Charlie, you know me. I'm just a poor mountain preacher."

"Poor or none, this is what you're gonna ride in."

Before them stood a Pullman trimmed in teak wood and brass. Gold-leaf lettering next to the door announced to all who saw it A.G. KING, PRESIDENT.

Rumford pulled open the door and led Lawless up the steps. Lawless loosened the muffler wrapped around his neck. "Pretty warm in here."

"The Pullman's got its own furnace. We've kept it stoked for the week it's been waiting on you." He laughed, wiggling a finger at a room in the corner. "We didn't want the Johnnie to freeze up."

"What's that car ahead?"

"Special, a baggage car. Preach, it goes with you. It's jammed with packages of I don't know what all. Came near to a half-day to load it."

A jolt shuddered through the car.

"Just the L&N hooking up," Rumford said. "They're ready to go, so I'll be saying goodbye to you now. At Maryville, the Little River will haul you on up."

Rumford hurried away, down the steps. He closed the door to keep December's blast outside.

The engine whistle sounded twice, then the engine belched. It jerked the train forward, throwing Lawless into an overstuffed couch. After he righted himself, he dumped his saddlebags and bedroll on the floor, and wallowed down in the comfort of the couch for the duration.

A short time later, the rhythmic clicking of the car's wheels over the rail joints slowed. Lawless peered out a window to see the train pulling through a switch and onto a sidetrack where it stopped.

Lawless pushed himself up. He went forward to the steps and the door and down to the snow-covered cinders outside. He shuffled up the line to watch the conductor wrestling a pin lock out of the coupler that hooked the baggage car to the L&N caboose.

The conductor pointed the pin at an engine and tender on the next sidetrack. "That rig's been idling there for two days, waiting for you. You must be one important man."

Before Lawless could let off with his rehearsed response, the conductor swung up on the steps of his caboose and waved to his engineer.

The L&N train yanked free of the baggage car and the Pullman. It glided away out onto the mainline and chuffed off, the acrid coal smoke lingering, causing Lawless's eyes to burn. The smell was no fun, either.

The waiting engine snorted to life. It rolled ahead, through a switch and onto the track where Lawless and his railcars stood. It slowed, then reversed, gathering speed as it rolled back.

Someone riding on the tender's rear knuckle wig-wagged his arm over his head to Lawless, the man with his collar pulled up around his ears and his cap pulled low against the cold.

Lawless waved back.

As the tender and engine drew closer, the railroader jumped from the knuckle and ran ahead. He twisted around and waved to his engineer to slow, then stop.

The knuckles of the tender and the baggage car touched and snapped together, and, as quickly, the railroader dropped a lock pin through, securing the coupling.

"Myron," Lawless asked, "that you?"

A face beamed out from beneath the bill of the striped cap. "Sure is, Preacher. We've been waitin' on ya."

"Who's up front? Swede?"

"Yup."

"Shouldn't you boys be working the log trains in the high mountains?"

"Snow's too deep. Old Man shut us down three days ago, sent us down here to wait on you. Must be mighty important, huh, Preach?"

"Can't be me."

"Preachahhhh!" bellowed a giant crunching through the snow, a giant whose beard was luxurious as Lawless's.

"Swede!"

The big men fell together in a bear hug.

"The Old Man wouldn't tell me what ta hell this is about, just said he wanted you ta hell up in Townsend before nightfall today. Gave Myron and me the Pacific 'cause it's got the speed."

"I'm impressed," Lawless said.

"All trains are to pull off and let you by. Want to ride up front?"

"Swede, you know what's back there in Mister King's car?"

"Been in it a time or two."

"There's a kitchen back there, and it's stocked like one of them high-class restaurants. There's a beef roast back there I been warming."

Swede Olsen leaned back. He clapped Lawless on the shoulders. "Hot sammiches!"

The trio of old friends clomped back to the president's car and climbed aboard. There in the galley, amid the smells of beef, baby Swiss cheese, and coffee, they made themselves a man-sized pile of sandwiches. They also filled a jug with prime brew and helped themselves to some of A.G. King's china cups, then went forward to the engine.

After the trio settled themselves in the cab of the Baldwin Pacific, Olsen hauled down on his whistle cord, a signal to the Maryville telegrapher to send the message up the line to Walland and Townsend, telling the stationmasters to divert all trains, that the special now rolling out onto the mainline had the high ball.

Olsen pushed the speed of the Pacific up to fifty-five miles an hour by the time the train roared into the first cut at Melrose. The great engine pulled down to forty on the grade.

It picked up speed again as it rolled out near Walland, then slowed to thirty-five on the climb along the side of Hurricane Mountain. It picked up again at Kinzel Springs and thundered across the Nawger bridge—the hanging bridge where, a decade before, an angry mob had lynched a man who had murdered his wife.

Olsen hauled back on the throttle and let the Pacific coast on into Townsend, braking only the last quarter-mile. Ahead, bathed in the engine's headlight, a dozen people milled around on the station's platform, among them, Lawless could see, A.G. King, and next to him, in a red outfit fringed in white, his wife.

"Some reception, huh, Preacher?" Olsen asked as he prodded Lawless toward the ladder and the snow below.

"Surely can't be for me."

"Now why not? And don't give me that 'I'm just a poor mountain preacher' bidness."

Lawless, puzzled, worked his way down from the Pacific's high cab. Before his boots touched the snow and the cinders beneath, King had his gloved hand out. "Reverend Lawless, I believe?"

"Call me Mister, Mister Lawless. I put my pants on one leg at a time, just like everybody else." He clasped King's hand and found himself having to hang on hard as King pumped away. To the side stood Cleta King, her smile as large as her husband's.

"Come in the station," King said. "I want to show you what you're going to do." He pushed Lawless up on the platform and through the door, to the ticket counter on which was spread a map. "Know what's in the baggage car you brought up?"

"Not the slightest." Lawless blew into his cupped hands to warm them.

Cleta King gazed up at him, her eyes bright. "Christmas."

"Pardon?"

"Christmas, Mister Lawless," King repeated. He put his arm around his wife's waist and gave her a smart hug. "Cleta here emptied Mister Proffitt's stores from Chattanooga to Bristol for the Santa Claus Train."

Lawless scrunched up his face.

"Don't you understand?" King asked.

Lawless shook his head.

"The country's been in a depression for years, and we've all felt it. But I didn't know how bad it was for our people until Cleta told me what you showed her at Higdon Camp. On my orders, my superintendents and foremen have drawn up lists. You, Mister Lawless, are going to take Christmas to everybody we can get to in the mountains, at least that part we control."

Cleta King put a hand on Lawless's arm. "A lot of people will meet the train, but some can't get out. Our foremen will take Christmas to them."

Lawless shook his head again. "I'm sorry, I don't like to be the one to dump a bucket of cold snow on a good idea, but these are proud people. They don't take to charity, I already told you that, particularly from rich people they see as having raped their mountains."

"You don't understand," King said. "This isn't coming from us. We want no credit. We don't even want our names mentioned. My superintendents and my foremen are to tell everyone this is from you. For one day, Mister Lawless, you get to be Santa Claus to what, two-, three-thousand people? Think about it, wasn't the original Saint Nicholas just like you, a preacher?"

A smile niggled at Lawless's mouth.

"Look at the map." King traced the railroad's trackage with his gloved finger. "We put plows on the front of our engines, and our engineers have been running up and down each branch line, pushing snow off the tracks. Tomorrow morning sunup, you, The Swede, Myron, and a crew in the baggage car leave here, and you stop anywhere you see somebody beside the track. You see they get what they need and go on."

Cleta King picked up the conversation. "Some of the people will be foremen. They'll have teams of horses and cutters. After they fill their lists, they'll drive back into the deep hollows."

"A truck will meet you where you spur off to Tremont," King said. "The driver will get a load to take on up to Elkmont. If we've done our work right, by sundown there shouldn't be a family in the Little River district that won't have Christmas."

"Well, praise God."

Cleta King slipped an arm through Lawless's. "Mister Lawless, my husband and I have a house full of guests who've been waiting for you since we sent word you were on your way. Would you hold a church service for us?"

****

Lawless found it as Cleta King had said, the front parlor and music room of the Kings' Octagon House stuffed with people, elbow to elbow, and more arriving.

"Is that the Todds there?" he asked.

"I sent Jamie to invite them."

"Preacher Todd," Lawless called out to a couple coming up the steps to the front porch.

"Mister Lawless!"

Lawless stepped forward and pumped the Baptist minister's hand.

"I came to hear you sermonize," Todd said.

"Believe me, Preacher, I don't like poachin' in your territory."

"You're not poaching. You may be a Methodist, but we both work for the same Lord."

"Hallelujah, brother."

"Any way I can help?"

"Yessir, if you'd read from the Good Book."

"I'd be honored."

Jamie, a boy of about eight, came up beside Lawless. "Can I take your saddlebags and your coat?" he asked.

"Jamie!" Lawless knelt down and wrapped his arms around the boy. "How is the best man I know?"

"Mighty fine. Haven't seen you since summer, Mister Lawless."

"Reach in my pocket, boy. See what you can find."

Delight danced on the child's face as he plunged his hand into the pocket of Lawless's mackinaw, so deep the coat swallowed his hand and arm up to his elbow. Up and out came the elbow, arm, hand and fingers, and, in the fingers, two smooth-sanded, red-lacquered circles of wood with a string wound around a peg between them.

"A yo-yo!"

"Saw that in a store down in Knoxville and knew there was a boy up here who'd just love to have it. Merry Christmas, Jamie."

"Thank you, Mister Lawless." The boy held the yo-yo up for the Kings to see. "Kin I show it to my ma, Mister King?"

"Absolutely. Jamie, you go along. I'll watch the front door for you."

The boy dashed inside, dodging around the legs standing between him and the kitchen.

"How did you know that's what he wanted?" Cleta King asked.

Lawless stood up. He stamped his feet to get the snow off his caulk boots. "I didn't. Jamie's a boy, just like me, only I'm a mite bigger."

"It was yours, wasn't it?"

"I can get another."

Inside, a woman took the Todds' and the Kings' coats and Lawless's mackinaw and saddlebags. She disappeared with them into a side room.

The Kings guided their guest from room to room, introducing him to people. To Lawless, half were strangers, but others were long-time friends–Harold and Homer Wright, Abraham Isaac Mulqueen, Jeff and Mabel Wilhite, and Gumble Jones and his wife, Lily.

"Boggs Kuhfuss!" he bellowed when he saw a fellow mountaineer across the room, at the far side of the front parlor. "You are forever from home!"

The two men pushed their way into the center where they hugged and clapped one another on the back.

"Everybody!" Lawless called out. "I want you to meet one of my deacons from deep in the high back country, way back up in Fish Camp. His name's Boggs Kuhfuss."

Kuhfuss blushed, apparently ill at ease in his work trousers and shirt of homespun among this gathering of men in suits and women in gowns and fine dresses.

Lawless worked Kuhfuss off into a corner. "Boggs, what are you doing this far from home?"

"Missus King sent word something special was planned, asked me to come. So I said my goodbyes to the family and walked out to Stringtown. They sent me the rest of the way on a donkey engine."

Cleta King interrupted them. "Mister Lawless, people want to hear from you."

"Boggs, I've gotta work for my supper. Would you excuse me?"

Kuhfuss bobbed his head.

Missus King guided Lawless to the opening between the music room and the front parlor. There she motioned for people to take seats. Men who didn't get chairs lounged against back walls or leaned against doorjambs. She handed Lawless his Bible from his saddlebags.

"Mister Lawless has agreed to favor us with a few words of the season," she said to her guests.

Lawless paged into his Bible. "A few words is a hard order for a preacher. Reverend Todd is here and, between us, we usually go for two hours."

Nervous laughter came from several people.

"Ahh, here it is," Lawless said as he stopped on a particular page. "The good reverend has agreed to help me. Would you read this?" He held the heavy Bible out to his fellow pastor.

Todd pushed his glasses up. He tapped a finger on a verse. "This one? Are you sure?"

"Uh-huh."

"All right. 'Jesus was born in the town of Bethlehem in Judea, during the time Herod was king. Soon afterward, some men who studied the stars came from the East to Jerusalem and asked, 'Where is the baby born to be king of the Jews? We saw his star when it came up in the east, and we have come to worship him—'"

Lawless touched Todd's arm. "That's far enough."

Todd closed the Bible.

Lawless caught sight of Jamie and waved him over.

The boy came. He put his hand in Lawless's hand.

"Know the story of the three kings, Jamie?"

"I do. They brought gifts to the baby Jesus."

"Why do you s'pose they did that?"

"They thought the baby Jesus was like them, a king."

"You're a smart one, Jamie. I bet your ma is proud of you."

"Yessir, she is."

Surprised laughter rippled through the rooms.

"Jamie, let me ask you one more question. Do you suppose those kings, those scholars, the Bible says, those rich men, were surprised where this baby king was?"

"I don't know."

Lawless caught the boy under the arms and swung him up to stand on a hard chair beside him. "Well, let's see if you and me can figure this thing out."

He put his arm around the boy's shoulders and turned, now, more to the adults in the rooms. "I been thinking about it, Jamie, and I think those rich kings expected to find the baby Jesus in a house kind of like this. You work here. It's pretty fancy, pretty nice, wouldn't you say?"

The boy grinned.

"But you and I know those kings didn't find Jesus in a nice house. No, they had to go around back to an old stable, a kind of a barn, kind of like Mister Mulqueen has behind his blacksmith shop where I sometimes leave my horse. Those kings, why they surely must have thought they'd made a mistake, got the wrong place, maybe even the wrong town, don't you think, Jamie?"

"I s'pose."

"But God must have said to them, 'Look up there.'" Lawless gestured to the corner of the ceiling. "And they did. And He must have said, 'See that star I put up there in the sky, shining down on this very spot? You got the right place. Go on in.'

"They must have been convinced because they did. And, my, were they ever happy. The Bible says 'What joy was theirs.' And those wise old kings, Jamie, they fell down on their prayer bones, and they worshiped the little baby. Do you remember what they did next?"

"They gave Jesus gifts."

"Remember what they were?"

"Gold and frankin-something and something."

"I don't always remember either. That's all right. The giving of gifts to Jesus, Jamie, I think this is the most important part of the story," Lawless went on. "These strangers, these kings, gave this little baby they didn't know, yet were convinced was the most important little boy in all the world, they gave him the very best they had, gold, frankincense, and myrrh. And, Jamie, that's the lesson for all of us here. We should give Jesus the very best that we have because God put Him here, His baby Son, to save us for a better life and a better world. That was awful nice of God, and somehow those rich old kings, they understood that."

Lawless peered into the boy's face. "S'pose we ought to pray?"

"Yes."

"Do you want to lead?"

"No."

A little laughter came from those nearest, those who heard the boy.

"That's all right." Lawless winked at Jamie before he bowed his head. "Great and powerful and loving God, I thank You for the faith of this little boy. May we each of us be like him, and like him, may we remember that it was another little boy, almost two thousand years ago, who was the center of this Christmastime celebration. I thank You for all who can give to Him, knowing full well that whatever those gifts are, somehow they will be used to advance Your work here among Your people whom You love so much. All glory to You, dear God. Amen."

Preacher Todd started it, and the Wright brothers joined in, then others . . .

> *We three Kings of Orient are,*
> *Bearing gifts we traverse afar,*
> *Field and fountain, moor and mountain . . .*

That flowed into . . .

> *Good King Wenceslas looked out*
> *On the Feast of Stephen . . .*

When Cleta King called out that everyone should go into the dining rooms for something to eat, Lawless hoisted Jamie to his shoulders and led the way in search of the wassail bowl and a cup of hot punch.

A.G. King came over to Boggs Kuhfuss hanging back. "Mister Kuhfuss, you're a guest. Come with me."

"No, I couldn't."

"No's are not heard in this house." King put a hand behind Kuhfuss's back and pushed the mountain man along. When they got to the serving table, King put an English bone-china plate in Kuhfuss's rough, chapped hands and loaded the plate with ham, breast of goose, potatoes, candied carrots, candied beets, sage stuffing, fruit salad, Christmas bread, and a slab of marble cake.

It took some time for Kuhfuss to clear his plate, but when he had done it, there King stood, urging him to go back for more.

Kuhfuss waved both hands to ward his host off, but did take another cup of hot rum punch.

****

At midnight, Lawless and Kuhfuss trudged up to the third-floor bedroom where Cleta King had sent their belongings. It seemed to Lawless that he had hardly turned out the light and hauled the quilts over his head that a rapping came at the door.

"Four-thirty," Jamie called into the bedroom. "Missus King says I should tell you the Christmas Train leaves in an hour. Ma's making breakfast."

Lawless pulled on his britches and shirt. He splashed cold water in his face and was ready to go when Kuhfuss let out with a "hooeee" as he peered at his face in the mirror.

"What?" Lawless asked.

"Think I better scrape these whiskers off."

Lawless flopped back on his bed. "While you do, guess I'll read some." He propped his Bible on his chest and paged into the Book of Thessalonians.

Kuhfuss hummed while he whipped up a lather in a soap cup. He continued humming as he spread the bubbles across his face and under his chin. That done, the mountaineer reached for his straight razor. He opened the blade to do the deed, only to be interrupted by a deep, raspy snoring–Lawless asleep, his Bible laying open on his chest.

****

Lawless and Kuhfuss pattered into the dining room to find Cleta King waiting for them, the table well covered with steaming bowls of oatmeal and platters of hot pancakes, ham and fried eggs, and three place settings. Jamie glanced up from his job of filling mugs with coffee.

Lawless clapped his hands together. "Boggs, you and me thought last night's feast was something, but look at this."

"Mister Lawless," Cleta King said from her place at the side of the table, "you and Mister Kuhfuss will need every bit of this breakfast for the day you have ahead of you."

"No doubt, Missus King, no doubt." Lawless sat down. He motioned Kuhfuss to the remaining chair. "Suppose we bless this."

He reached for Cleta King's and Kuhfuss's hands as he bowed his head. "Gracious Lord, we thank You for this wonderful food and Jamie's momma who prepared it. It will warm us and fill us and carry us nigh unto noon. Amen."

Lawless glanced up to find Jamie by his side, setting a mug of coffee at his place.

Cleta King stirred a spoonful of sugar into her coffee. "Mister Lawless."

He reached for a pitcher of cream for his oatmeal.

"The baggage car contains bins marked 'men,' 'women,' 'boys,' 'girls' and one marked 'babies.' Each item is wrapped. All you and the helpers need to do is be sure you give out the right number of things to the people and our foremen at each stop."

"We can do that, can't we, Boggs?" Lawless said as he handed the cream pitcher to his fellow mountaineer.

"There's also a bin marked 'quilts' and one marked 'hams.' Give them out to those you know who are most in need. And remember, not a word where this came from."

Lawless helped himself to the fried eggs. "You coming with us?"

"No, my job's here. I'm going to help Missus Mapes get things ready for Christmas dinner. We have a trainload of children coming up from the Knoxville orphanage for the day."

"Really?"

"Isn't that amazing, Mister Lawless? All the years Mister King and I have been married, we've been without children, except for Jamie when his mother came to work for us. Tomorrow, Octagon House will be bursting with them."

"Nothing like family, is there, Missus King?" Kuhfuss said.

"No, there is nothing as sweet as family. You'll come back and be with us, won't you, Mister Lawless?"

"Missus King, I got family scattered all over these mountains. I thank you for the invite, but I really should be with them." He handed the platter of pancakes across the table to Kuhfuss.

Kuhfuss forked a stack onto his plate. "Missus King, Preacher's gonna be with me an' my family. My Lizzy, she said she's gonna have a hind quarter of deer meat roastin' over the fire for Preach an' our children."

****

Only after the last sausage had been put down did Lawless and Kuhfuss push away from the table.

Jamie stood nearby with their outdoor gear and Lawless's saddlebags and bedroll.

The men shagged themselves into their mackinaws and slapped caps on their heads.

At the door, with a dust of snow blowing in, Lawless took Cleta King's hands in his. He gazed for a long moment into her eyes. "You're a blessing, Missus King. You really are."

"No, what you do is the blessing. I'm just glad I can help. Come back soon?"

"Surely before spring."

She took a small package from the stand by the door and pressed it into Lawless's hand.

He found himself struggling for a voice. "I don't have anything for you."

"You have no idea how much you've given me. Now go or you'll miss the train."

****

The Swede, in a red coat and a red earlapper cap, gave two sharp blasts on the Pacific's whistle when he saw Lawless and Kuhfuss making their way toward his train in the gloom that precedes dawn. He leaned out the window of his cab. "I look a little bit like old Sandy Claus, don't I?" he hollered.

Lawless gave a hitch to his saddlebags on his shoulder. "Your whiskers need to be white."

Olsen fluffed up his beard. "I expect they will be soon enough, Preach."

Three lumber trucks, each with a load of packages in canvas sacks, rumbled away from the baggage car. Lawless let his gaze follow them. "Swede, where they going?"

"One is headed to the backside of Townsend . We got us a lot mill and railroad workers livin' there with their families. Second there is goin' to Nawger Knob, Kinsel Springs, and Matthew's Mountain,. The third's got the long drive to Laurel Valley and Rich Mountain Gap."

"Cade's Cove?"

"That truck, too. We got us six families out there. The driver an' helper promised the Old Man they'd walk in if they have to, to get to 'em. You boys better get in the baggage car. We're ready to roll."

Lawless found Roy Eagle Clark and Clyde Henthorne, Olsen's brakeman and conductor, lounging in the doorway of the baggage car. The men reached down and hauled Lawless and Kuhfuss up.

"Merry Christmas, Preacher," Roy Eagle said as he rolled the door closed. "Ready to do this thang?"

"If you be, Roy Eagle."

The baggage car jounced as the engineer put power to the Pacific.

Roy Eagle took down a clipboard. "Preach, we got us a system worked out. One toot from Swede means he's got people on the left side of the train, and we open that door and load 'em up. Two toots means the people's on the right."

Eagle, a skinny, knot-hard mountain farmer—hawk-nosed and tall, like Lawless some six-foot-two—a decade ago had picked up a crosscut saw to work for the lumber company. He and a partner had cut around Jake's Creek for several years when a tree they were felling kicked back. It caught his partner in the side of the head, killing him.

Eagle wrapped his partner in a tarp, lifted him on his shoulder, and packed him six miles through Bearpen Gap, over Timber Ridge, and down to Green Camp where the man's mother lived. He dug the grave and helped the old woman bury her son. Then he walked out of the woods and demanded a safe job. He had been a brakeman ever since.

Lawless hopped his fanny up on the baggage counter. "How's the wife doing, Roy Eagle?"

"Tolerable, tolerable."

Henthorne looked over from the lists on the baggage clerk's desk. "Didja know Roy Eagle and Mary Lynne got themselves a new baby?"

"No, when?"

"Thanksgiving week."

"What's that, six now, Roy Eagle?" Lawless asked.

"Yessir." He dug in his pocket for his cigarette papers and tobacco bag, to roll a smoke.

"Isn't it about time you quit making children?"

"Not 'til we got us nine, Mary Lynne says. Personally, I'd like an even dozen. Mary Lynne says I'm the big-family type. It's true. Poppie and Mommie, they had sixteen of us before they called it quits."

The train slowed and two toots sounded.

Roy Eagle stepped over to the door on the right side of the car. He rolled the door open and leaned out. "Oh, my golly, we got us a gaggle of people."

"Anybody we know?" Henthorne asked.

"I see our foreman there with a cutter, but them other folks, they be strangers to me."

The train stopped in front of the group huddled together by a junction with an abandoned sidetrack. The foreman, bundled in a bearskin coat, handed his list up, and Henthorne and Roy Eagle set to bagging packages.

Lawless jumped down.

"Hey-dee," a man said. "Who you?"

"Preacher Lawless."

"I've heered about you. You've not come our way."

"If you're inviting, I'll be there. But it may be February."

"You be welcome to hold church in our house. I'm Ben Thistledown." He shook hands with Lawless. "You'll find my fambley at the edge of Wildcat Flats. Know where that is, a hike up that abandoned spur?"

"I'll find it. You got my promise."

"Is this the Sandy Train we heered about?"

"Sure is. How many families you got up there at Wildcat?"

"Seven. And an old man and his woman what live up a side hollow."

"What's the breakdown—men, women, boys, girls, and babies?"

Thistledown turned to the others in his group. "Let's see, whadda we got, eleven men and maybe thirteen women when you count in the older children." He looked to a girl in a thin coat and scarf. "What say, Sallie, for little ones? Four boys maybe, three girls, and don't forget there's that new baby."

She gave a weak smile.

"Yeah, Preacher, that's it," Thistledown said.

Lawless hoisted himself back up into the baggage car where he and Kuhfuss bagged the order. They put in four hams and two quilts for good measure.

In a corner, Lawless found a bushel of oranges. He stuffed one in his coat pocket. He and Kuhfuss then handed down the bags filled to overflowing to the waiting arms of the men.

"Sallie," Lawless called out. He held up the orange. "For you."

He tossed it to the girl.

She caught it with both hands and brought it up to her nose. She sniffed it, then held the orange up for her father to see. Thistledown patted her face.

The girl turned to Lawless. "Thank you, mister. Merry Christmas."

The train began to roll. Lawless stood in the doorway of the baggage car, his gaze locked on the girl's wan face. He waved and she waved until the train rounded a bend and Lawless lost sight of the child. How many hours had she waited for the Santa Claus Train in the cold and the snow? He didn't know.

It ran that way for the next six miles, the engineer stopping every half-mile or so when he saw people standing beside the tracks, people who, like those from Wildcat Flats, had heard a Christmas train was coming. The longest stop came at a junction with a road that climbed up to Elkmont. It took forty-five minutes to bag the orders and load them on a waiting lumber truck.

The train dead-ended at Stringtown at noon. The Little River foreman, who lived there, had a hot meal waiting. Santa's helpers ate, but only after they made sure each family at the end of the line had something from the baggage car.

"Mister Kuhfuss, you going on home?" The Swede asked during a pause in his shoveling of mashed potatoes into his mouth.

"This is the closest I'm going to get. Guess I better."

The engineer reached for a biscuit. "Preacher, I'd like to keep you with me, but why don't you go on with Mister Kuhfuss?"

"What about the families up Mark's Cove and Blowdown?"

"Don't you worry. The boys and me, we'll back down to Tremont, then run up the spur lines to 'em. We'll see they're cared for." Olsen speared a chicken leg from a passing platter. "And Mister Kuhfuss, don't you worry none about your folks or those up in Peawood and Higdon-town. I expect a cutter has got through from Elkmont by now and made the rounds."

Lawless and Kuhfuss cleaned their plates down to the shine before they pulled on their coats and went back to the baggage car for their gear. There Lawless gathered up more than his saddlebags and bedroll. He took six oranges from the dwindling bushel. He stuffed them inside his shirt to keep them from freezing and tucked a quilt under his arm.

Lawless and Kuhfuss made their goodbyes to Henthorne, Roy Eagle, Myron the fireman, and The

Swede, then set out to the east. They had hardly gotten across Stringtown's frozen creek when they were kicking through snow up to their knees. Lawless took the first turn at breaking trail. They switched off throughout the afternoon, and, by five o'clock, they stood atop a hillock across from the Fish Camp schoolhouse.

Kuhfuss let out a sharp whistle. His dog, bedded down at the front door, raised his head. When he heard the whistle repeated, he bolted into the road, plowing a turn as he raced off in the direction of the whistling—howling and barking—leaping through the deepest snow. Kuhfuss caught him up as he would a child, the dog wriggling and sworping his tongue at Kuhfuss's face.

Lawless laughed. "Some sight there, Boggs."

"Miss me, boy?" Kuhfuss asked the dog. He wrenched his head away, to avoid a canine kiss. "Oh gawd, I got dog spit all over."

He put his dog down. "Looks like we're home, Preacher. Let's get ourselves up to the house and put our feet in front of the fire. Don't know 'bout you, but I'm chilled to the bone and wet clean through."

"Yeah, me, too."

The three pushed on down the hillock and across the creek. When they got to the road, they stepped into a track that had been made by a team of horses and a cutter.

People leaned out of doors, shouting their hellos. Kuhfuss and Lawless waved back.

"Didja hear," a man called out, "we got the lease from the national park?"

"No!" Kuhfuss called back.

"It's true! Mister Hansen, he brought it up today. Said for it to be legal, we had to pay something. So I give him a dollar."

Kuhfuss waved, and he and Lawless continued on. "Isn't that somethin'? We got us the lease for the hospital land. How do you s'pose that come about?"

Lawless pointed up.

Kuhfuss grinned. "Yup, I'd say yer right. It's a Christmas miracle."

At the front gate of the Kuhfuss place stood the home greeting committee, Kuhfuss's children stamping in the snow and flapping their arms against the cold. Little Gracie and Lucinda, all giggles, reached out for their father's hands. They pulled him on toward the house while Matthew Lee and Bethy Anne took Lawless in tow.

The thunder of multiple pairs of feet on the porch, stamping snow from their shoes and boots, brought the woman of the house to the door—Lizzy Kuhfuss. She threw her arms open, and Kuhfuss fell into them.

"You hear the news?" she asked.

"Indeed I did."

"It's a miracle, isn't it?"

****

As darkness stole across Fish Camp, neighbors came to the Kuhfuss house expecting a Christmas Eve service, all except for one family. Word was that Missus Stamps was ailing and didn't want to brave the cold.

At Christmas Eve service, Lawless hadn't thought a thing about it. He was padding around in his stockinged feet, enjoying his enameled cup of hot chocolate and the aroma of the fresh-cut pine boughs Lizzy Kuhfuss had put on the mantle above the fireplace, when Tyler Keegan bounded through the door ahead of his parents, shouting to Lawless, "What story you got for us tonight?"

Lawless waited for all the families to shuck themselves out of their winter coats and boots and settle around the room before he took up his Bible. He let it fall open and read the first verse that came to his eye. Lawless shook his head. He opened the book to another section.

"Now here's a verse I like." He crooked a finger at Ty Keegan. The boy came over, and Lawless set him in his lap and held the Bible for him. "Verse eight," he whispered in the boy's ear.

"'There were some shepherds in that part of the country who were spe . . . spe–'"

"Spending," Lawless said.

"'–spending the night in the fields taking care of their flocks. An angel of the Lord ap . . . ap–'"

"Appeared."

"'–to them, and the glory of the Lord showed over them. They were–' What's that word?" Tyler glanced up at Lawless.

"Terribly."

"'–terribly afraid, but the angel said to them, 'Do not be afraid. I bring you good tidings of great joy that shall be to all people. This day in David's town your–'"

"Savior."

"'–your savior was born, Christ the Lord.'"

"Now go down to here." Lawless touched a verse further down the page.

A furrow formed between Tyler's brows as he concentrated on the new words. "'Suddenly a great army of heaven's angels appeared with the angel, singing pa– praises to God. 'Glory to God in the–'"

"Highest."

"'–heaven, and peace on earth to those with whom he is pa–pa–pleased.'"

Lawless hugged the boy. "Thank you, Ty. I expect your ma wants you back, don't you think?"

Tyler Keegan slipped down from Lawless's lap and worked his way around the multiple pairs of knees separating him from his mother. She pulled him to her side. There he leaned his head against her shoulder.

"Reason I like this part of the Christmas story," Lawless said as he laid his Bible on the hearth, "God sent His messenger to shepherds, people like you, hill farmers who wrestled a living from the soil, people who didn't have anything more than the land God gave them. And that radiant angel gave those old shepherds the good news–'God's little baby Son is born among you, just down the road a piece, in Bethlehem town, you'll find him there.' And they did. We know that because Luke, the fine gospel writer, tells us that a little later on. You remember that?" Lawless gestured to Tipton Seabolt, the community's patriarch, sitting with his wife by the back wall.

"I surely do," Seabolt said.

"Knew you would. Nobody's better with his Bible than Tip. Mary and Joseph were amazed by what the shepherds told. And the shepherds were amazed, too, because it was all true what the angel had said. Says Luke, 'The shepherds went back to the fields, singing praises to God for all they had heard and seen. It had been just as the angel had told them.'"

Seabolt raised a hand. "Excuse me, Preacher, but I've always felt the really important part is back there in the song those angels sang, 'Glory to God in the highest of heavens and peace on earth to those with whom He is well pleased.'"

Lawless shot his fist up. "Amen, brother. You are the ones with whom God is well pleased, you, the descendants of the shepherds, you hill farmers, you who love this land that God gave you, and take care of it, you who love the families He gave you and love your neighbors, whom He also gave you. You love them and take care of them.

"So I expect the angels are up there gathered around God's broad shoulders, singing about you tonight. I want you to remember that because, like those shepherds of olden times, you are God's special people."

Lawless closed his eyes. He hummed, then sang . . .

Oh, come all ye faithful, joyful and triumphant,
Oh, come ye, oh, come ye to Bethlehem . . .

Voices around the room picked up the melody. That carol blended into . . .

Oh, little town of Bethlehem!
How still we see thee lie . . .

And . . .

Silent night! Holy night!
All is calm, all is bright,
Round yon Virgin Mother and Child,
Holy Infant, so tender and mild,
Sleep in heavenly peace, sleep in heavenly peace.

****

Lawless excused himself when it appeared that the Fish Camp neighbors intended to talk long into the night. "Boggs," he said, "I'd like to take communion up to the Stampses since they couldn't come out."

"I'll come with ya."

"No, you done enough for the day. You'd be better to stay with your family."

Tyler Keegan, Lawless's Bible reader, tugged on his sleeve.

The peacher looked down at his young assistant. "What is it, boy?"

"Kin I come?"

"Well, now," he said, winking at Kuhfuss, "you've been right handy tonight. Suppose you go ask your pa."

Ty raced across the room to where his parents were visiting with the Clabos. "Pa! Pa! Kin I go with the preacher?"

Wendell Keegan put a hand on his boy's head. "Son, what's this about?"

"Preacher said he's gonna take communion up to Missus Stamps. He said I could help him if you'll let me."

Keegan turned his gaze from his son to Lawless on the other side of the room. Lawless gave an okay sign.

Keegan swivelled to his wife. "Hon, what do you think?"

Nan Keegan knelt before Tyler. She put her hands on his shoulders and looked deep into his eyes. "You really want to do this, don'tcha?"

A big smile answered, a smile that revealed a chipped tooth.

"Well, I can't think of anybody I'd rather have you with. Let's get you snugged up."

Snugging up included a long coat, galoshes, a knit cap that Nan Keegan pulled down over Tyler's ears, mittens, and a scarf that, when she wrapped it around the boy's throat and up over his chin and nose, let nothing more than his eyes be seen.

Lawless sat on the hearth, pulling on his knee-high caulk boots. When he got them laced up, he went after his mackinaw and his battered railroad cap. Next he put bread and a fruit jar of wine in his saddlebag. Lawless snatched up a package he had earlier wrapped in butcher paper, hefted his saddlebags to his shoulder, and, with the boy hanging onto his gloved hand, pushed out into the night.

Tyler Keegan's dog bounded out when the boy and the preacher came by the Keegans' house. The dog took his master's mittened hand in his mouth and walked along beside him.

"Purty night, isn't it?" Tyler said, gazing up at Lawless, the scarf muffling his words.

"Surely is. We got all the stars out."

"Whatcha want me to do when we get to the Stampses?"

"Fetch and carry. How about that?"

"I kin do that."

They went on, the only sound that of snow crunching beneath their boots.

At the high end of the hollow, they came to the Stamps cabin. Lawless knocked on the door.

A girl opened it. "Ma's got a fearsome cold," she said as she stood there, peering out at the callers. "Won't you come in? I know she'd like to see you."

The girl—Jenny—led Lawless and the boy back to the lean-to kitchen where her mother sat in a straight-back chair by the stove, wrapped to her chin in a thin-worn quilt, the room stuffy and pungent, smelling of a homemade cold salve. Children sat around the table, playing with cornhusk dolls, all except for a small boy, a three-year-old—Fredrick Jackson. He laid on a blanket on the floor, curled up asleep, a half-dozen unopened packages nearby.

Missus Stamps reached out a quaking hand.

Lawless took it. "It's good to see you, Missus Stamps. Missed you and your brood at church, so Tyler here and me thought we'd bring a little church to you."

Missus Stamps choked back a cough. "Fraid I'm feelin' a bit puny."

"I see by the packages old Santy Claus has been by."

"We're keepin' them to open tomorrow. T'was a real sweet surprise when them men come by. Children can't hardly wait to tear into 'em."

"Isn't Christmastime wonderful?"

"It surely is, Mister Lawless."

"Would you and Jenny like communion?"

Missus Stamps sniffled back a tear. "Been a long time. It's a right wonder. Jenny, would you git a chair for Mister Lawless? And hush the children?"

"Tell you what," Lawless said as he settled on the chair the girl brought to him, "why don't we make them a part of this?"

He motioned for the children to gather round. They sat on the plank floor except the four-year-old, Millie. She leaned on her mother's lap, twisting on her bare toes.

"Got the Bible there, Ty?" Lawless asked his assistant.

With both hands, the boy pulled the great, heavy book from the saddlebag and handed it on.

Lawless opened it to the page from which Tyler had earlier read. Then he turned one more page. "Ty read the shepherds' story of Christmas for us down there at the Kuhfusses. What say Jenny reads us about Simeon?"

She gazed at her mother. She gave a nod, and the girl came over. She leaned on Lawless's shoulder. "This one?" she asking, touching a fingertip to the verse.

"That's right."

"'At that time, there was a man named Simeon living in Jerusalem,'" she read. "'He was a good, God-fearing man and was waiting for Israel to be saved. The Holy Spirit was with him and had assured him he would not die before he had seen the Lord's promised Messiah. Led by the Spirit, Simeon went into the temple. When the parents brought the child Jesus to the Temple to do for him what the Law required, Simeon took the child in his arms and gave thanks to God. 'Now, Lord, You have kept Your promise, and You may let Your servant go in peace. With mine own eyes I have seen Your salvation.'"

"Thank you, Jenny." Lawless took Missus Stamps's hands in his. He gazed into her eyes. "The birth of a child is a happy time, it's new life—new life and hope. And that's what's right here at the center of Christmastime, a little baby boy and a very special hope for each of us.

"Old Simeon, there, he didn't meet that little baby until some years later, when the baby was partially growed—a man child. But he recognized him right off. He gathered him up in his arms, and he hugged him, and he thanked God for a promise kept." Lawless put an arm around Jenny's waist and she an arm around his neck. "'If I die now,' Simeon said, 'it's all right. I'm a happy man. I'm content because I have seen salvation.'

"I know you and Jenny have seen Jesus, and you've both been baptized into His spirit, and you can be content. That's the promise of Christmas."

Lawless took Jenny's hands. He joined them with her mother's and bowed his head. "Lord, bring blessings to this house for it contains Your special people. Amen."

Tyler brought a chalice out of the saddlebag, and Lawless, the fruit jar of wine. After he poured some into the chalice, he gave the jar to Tyler to cap and set on the floor.

"The Good Book says that whenever we gather together we are to remember Jesus and what He did to save us." Lawless then brought out the bread and unwrapped it. "This bread represents His body which was broken on the cross for us. Take, eat, and remember Him."

Missus Stamps and Jenny each tore a small piece from the loaf and put it in their mouths.

Lawless took the chalice that Tyler held. "In the same way, this wine stands for Jesus's blood which He willingly shed for our salvation. Drink of it and remember Him."

Each in turn sipped from the cup.

Lawless poured the remaining wine back into the fruit jar, then wiped the chalice dry with a towel from his saddlebag. He wrapped the chalice and gave it to Tyler to pack away, motioning toward the bread and the fruit jar, that the boy should pack them as well.

Lawless leaned down to the children at his feet. "You been so good tonight, I got something for you." He winked at little Samantha Jane who had hung on his every word. He reached inside his shirt and brought out three large oranges and then three more. He placed one in the hands of each child and one in Missus Stamps's hands. To Jenny, he said, "The extra one, that's for Fredrick Jackson, for when he wakes up in the morning."

He beckoned to Tyler. The boy came to Missus Stamps. He laid a butcher paper-wrapped package on her lap.

She fumbled with the paper, her eyes filling with wonder as Jenny helped her open the package.

Missus Stamps gasped. "Jenny, isn't it the purtiest?"

Missus Stamps's children, like bees in a hive, clustered in tight. They ran their hands over the gift.

"It's the wonderfullest quilt, Mister Lawless. Who do I thank?"

"Thank God, Missus Stamps, thank God. It's Christmastime." He pulled Tyler in. "Ty, you been a good helper. Think we ought to be going?"

The boy went for Lawless's saddlebags. He hoisted them over his shoulder.

Lawless hugged each child and squeezed Missus Stamps's hands a last time. He made his way toward the door. Then he and Tyler were outside. Tyler's dog roused himself from where he had been curled in a tight ball against the wall of the cabin, his tail over his nose.

As they stepped out into the yard, Lawless gazed up into the cloudless night sky, at the stars showered out like diamonds. "Ty, what say we men go for a walk? There's a special place beyond the head of the hollow—know you've seen it a hunnerd times—but you've never seen it like it is tonight."

He reached down for the boy's hand, and the two and the dog gabbled along, wading through the snow, the snow becoming progressively deeper as they climbed up out of Fish Camp Hollow.

Sometime on, Ty, puffing hard, said, "I'm about done."

Lawless stopped. He swept his assistant, thigh deep in the snow, up onto his shoulders, his saddlebags, too. He pushed on, the dog following in Lawless's track. "See that stump ahead?"

"Yessir."

"That's our destination."

The stump, a chestnut, stood some four feet high, although only the upper two feet showed above the snow.

Lawless came up to it. He swept a portion of snow from the top of the stump with his arm, then set the boy in the cleared area. Tyler's dog whined, so Lawless lifted him up beside his master.

"What do you think, Ty, this old stump's, what, maybe six feet across?"

The boy measured it with his eye. "Could be."

"It must have been a mighty powerful, mighty big old tree. I'm sorry I never saw it. It was gone before I ever came by here."

"They took it before I was borned. Pa says everybody called it the Granddaddy Tree."

"I reckon it was. But the cutters left a nice tree over there." Lawless gave a nod toward a lone fir a dozen paces away. It looked to be about fifteen feet tall, its branches full, drooping under their winter burden.

"It is purty," Tyler said.

"Remember the story of the Christmas star?"

The boy leaned on Lawless, listening.

"It led the three wise men to where the baby Jesus was. When I come by here by night, I like to sit on this old stump and look off way up there." Lawless pointed with his gloved hand to a star high in the sky, brighter than the others. It glistened and appeared to wink.

"My daddy called it the compass star," Lawless said, "but I like to think of it as God's star because it's always there. And it always will be."

Mesmerized by the glittering canopy that swept from horizon to horizon, the two gazed upwards until time was lost to them . . .

The world is still tonight,
The world is old.
The stars around the fold do show their light,
And so did they a thousand years ago,
And so will they, good lad, when we lie cold.

Holly & Mistletoe

Will Click, a hard-muscled retired Air Force pilot, rested himself against the side of the U-Haul trailer while Scotty Moore, the poster image of a state police trooper except for his sweatshirt emblazoned with a shoe print and the words 'Knoxville Flatfeet,' fumbled with the key for the padlock.

"You know," Click said, "this is a gawd awful time to be moving, two days before Christmas."

"Divorce came through. No reason to stay up in Knoxville anymore."

"Yeah, and my girl didn't have anything to do with this."

Moore grinned at the mention. "Oh, I wouldn't say that didn't have something to do with deciding to move here rather than, say, Strawberry Plains."

He twisted the key in the lock. Moore pulled down when he felt the mechanism release and put the padlock in his pants pocket. He swung the trailer's double doors open.

Click came around. He peered inside. "That's it? That's all you got?"

"That's all the divorce left me."

"My gawd, looks like the junk dorm students put on the curb when spring semester's over."

Moore hauled out a Jack Daniels box filled with books. He hefted it to Click. "This is my dorm stuff."

"You never threw it away?"

"No chance. It went straight from the dorm to Barb's and my first apartment. Combined with her stuff, we called it old college, early matrimony."

"Jeez."

A head poked out from an upstairs window of a rambling two-story that had known sweeter times. "Scott?"

Moore swung around and peered up at the smudged face of AJ Garrison—Will Click's lawyer daughter—the sleeves of her UT sweatshirt bunched above her elbows. "Yeah?"

"Have you got any bleach?"

"No. Why?"

"You've got rust stains and mineral deposits in the bathroom sink and the toilet. The Comet won't take them out."

"Muriatic acid," Click whispered.

"How's that?"

"Muriatic acid. That's what you need. I got a jug at the house."

Moore hollered up to Garrison. "Your dad says muriatic acid! He's got some."

"You ready to bring your things in?"

"Yeah!"

"Well, put everything on the landing. I don't want you and Pop tracking up your clean floors."

Moore glanced at Click whose only response was a shrug.

"Right," Moore called out.

Garrison pulled back inside, and the window slid closed.

"Well, let's do it," Click said.

The 'everything' turned out to be eight liquor boxes of books, a pile of boards and bricks for a bookcase, a card table accompanied by four folding chairs, only two of which matched the table, a couch that sagged like a black bear had slept on it for an overly long winter, a plastic chair in the shape of a hand, a glass-topped coffee table, a Bush's Beans box labeled 'kitchen stuff,' a Corn Flakes case labeled 'bedroom stuff,' a Sugar Pops case labeled 'stuff stuff,' two suitcases, a gym bag, a rollaway bed, and a black-and-white TV with a coat hanger for an antenna. The two men schlepped it all inside and up the stairs, and stacked it on the second-floor landing in under forty-five minutes.

Moore opened the door to the flat only to hear Garrison's voice coming his way from back in the kitchen, "Take your shoes off before you come in here."

"She always so bossy?"

"Ever since she was a little kid. Mind of her own, always had to be in charge."

Moore settled on the top step. He unlaced his hiking boots. Click, on the arm of the couch, pulled off a shoe. He massaged his ankle.

"This is embarrassing," Moore said.

"What's that?"

He held up his foot. Two toes aired themselves through a hole in the end of his sock.

Click took off his other shoe. A toe poked its way into the light from the end of his sock. Click wiggled his toe, showing it off. "No wife to mend for me either."

Garrison bustled out onto the landing. She stared at her father and his holey sock, then gave a look of disdain to Moore's bare toes. "You two are the cheapest. I think you both could part with a dollar and a half for new socks."

Click admired his wiggling toe. "I'm on a pension."

"Took all my money," Moore said, "just to set up housekeeping here."

"Gawd." Garrison picked up the 'kitchen stuff' carton and huffed inside with it.

After a moment, Moore slapped Click's leg. "Well, let me give you the cook's tour."

The two rose and shuffled on into the flat in their stockinged feet, the first room smelling of Pine-sol and Pledge. Click's eyes widened. "My golly, Miss Molly, you could hold a square dance in here."

"Big, isn't it? I'm thinking of putting my grand pianah over there in front of the bay winder." Moore snickered.

"You're going to put your Christmas tree there," Garrison said from the kitchen.

"I don't have a Christmas tree!"

"Well, get one."

This time it was Moore who shrugged.

Click cocked his head to one side. His gaze fell on a fireplace that had rose tiling on the hearth and up the sides to a carved cherry mantelpiece. "That work, the fireplace?"

"You know, I never asked."

The oak floor gleamed with new wax Garrison had put down.

"Nice," Click said. "You have to do much work on the place?"

"AJ didn't tell you?"

"No, I've been away a lot. The charter business."

"Then you missed it all."

"I guess."

Moore patted a wall painted cream. "There was wallpaper here and in all the rooms–tired stuff, dirty up to waist high from the hands of little kids. I didn't mind it much, but AJ said I had to rent a steamer."

"Stripped the walls, huh?"

"Then we had to spackle the cracks in the plaster–lotta cracks–and we painted. But there was a benefit to it all."

"Yeah?"

"Missus Caudileski, my landlady, she liked what we did and knocked off half a month's rent."

Garrison's voice came from the kitchen. "Tell Pop about the light fixture."

Moore went to the middle of the room. He stood beneath a brass chandelier. "The light that was here, AJ thought it was too small, so Missus C goes rummaging in the basement, and she finds this chandelier. The three of us spent one evening polishing the brasswork and washing the globes. Then I wired it up, even put a dimmer on it."

Click admired the finished product. He chuckled about something he saw and, without saying anything, followed Moore back to the kitchen where they came on Garrison and Mabel Caudileski unpacking the 'kitchen stuff'.

"Missus C," Moore said, "I didn't know you were here."

She held up two State Police mugs. "This all you have for coffee?"

"Missus C, I'm a bachelor now."

"What are you going to do when you have company?"

"I guess I'll break out the straws."

"You're hopeless, young man, you know that?"

"Hopelessly in love with you."

"Don't I wish." She looked beyond Moore to Click. "I'm so glad to have this young man living above me. I didn't know who I'd find for a renter in the dead of winter, and him a policeman."

"A trooper," Garrison said. She picked three Melmac plates and a cereal bowl out of the 'stuff' box and placed them on a shelf.

"That's what I said, a policeman. Mister Moore—"

"I'd rather you call me Scotty."

Missus C touched a mug to the front of his sweatshirt. "Mister Scotty, I have to ask. What's Knoxville Flatfeet?"

"That was our baseball team—all Knoxville cops."

The eyebrows of the big-boned woman knitted together.

"Flat feet, get it?" Moore asked.

"Sorry, I don't."

"That's all right. All you need to know is we were good. We went twenty-eight and two in the summer league."

"It's a man thing," Garrison said to Missus C, the older woman in a misshapen house dress and lace-up shoes that came up over her ankles. "Scotty, show Pop your bedroom."

"All right. Will, we might as well set up the bed while we're at it."

He and Click went back to the front room, Moore hauling off his sweatshirt on the way. He shook it out and hung it and his cap on a coat tree that had curled arms. "Missus C loaned me this until I can get something of my own," he said of the tree. Moore ran his fingers back through his hair, strands of gray showing at the temples.

Click slipped out of his leather flight jacket. He hung it on one of the arms, but he kept his knit cap on.

On the landing, they picked up the bed—folded up and secure—and carried it on inside. In silent communication, they lifted it high so the wheels wouldn't mar the waxed floor. Moore guided to his right, into a short hallway, then through a door into a second, but smaller, front room—the bedroom.

He and Click positioned the bed before they unlatched the ends and let the frame and mattress fold out. Click sat on the bed—tested it—the springs making stretchy music beneath his bottom. "Not exactly quiet, is it?"

"It didn't keep me awake at college, though my roommate complained."

Click peered underneath. "How about you hook your radio antenna wire to the springs? I betcha you could get WSM out of Nashville—Grand Ol' Opry."

"You listen to that?"

"Sometimes. AJ thinks it's corn. But then I think some of the music she listens to is kinda strange. The Byrds—don't understand 'em—and Janis Joplin, all she does is scream."

Moore went to the side window. "Come look at this."

Click got up, and the bed's springs sproinged back. He joined Moore, gazing out. "East window, you're going to get the morning sun."

"Nice way to wake up, huh?"

Click gazed beyond the house and its side yard. "Hey, you can see up into the mountains from here."

"Well, Cullowhee at least." But Moore gestured toward a bare-branched tree much closer, just beyond the porch roof. "That's what I wanted you to see, that apple tree."

"Know what you got there?"

"Yes, an apple tree."

Click chuckled. "It's not just any apple tree. That's a Virginia Beauty. Fruit sweet like cherries."

"Really?"

"It's an old-timey apple. You're going to love the fruit from that tree."

"How do you know so much about it?"

"I used to help Mister Caudileski pick for part of the harvest. Virginia Beauties, good keepers. My wife wouldn't have anything else." Click rubbed the thick muscle between his neck and shoulder as memories came flowing up from the far reaches of his mind. "The old tree kind of got away after Mister C died. Maybe you should offer to prune it and spray it, bring it back into shape."

"Yes—well, what I wanted to tell you is what Missus C told me."

"Uh-huh?"

"This was her boys' room when they were kids."

"I can picture that."

"They'd sneak out at night—go out this window, cross the roof, and climb down that tree."

"Scotty, this is a great house for kids."

Moore jerked his jaw. He turned away to a door and opened it, pulled a chain on a bare-bulb light fixture. "Only closet on the second floor," he said. "Big enough, huh?"

"For what little you've got."

Moore pulled the chain again. That returned the closet to darkness. He led Click out and across the hall to the back bedroom. "I'm thinking of setting up my office here," he said, pointing to where things might go. "Put a door across a couple two-drawer files for a desk, I could write up my reports here, keep my law books over there. Did you know we get tested every six months on the statutes we're expected to enforce?"

"And I thought we commercial pilots had it tough."

"All of us troopers, we have a lot we have to read." Moore felt the padlock in his pocket. He pulled the lock out and went back to the closet where he parked the padlock and its key on a shelf.

"I go further than most," he said when he came back. "I read the court cases and the judges' opinions, particularly those from the state supreme court."

Click moved around this back bedroom-cum-office, springing on the balls of his feet, as if he were testing the soundness of the floor. He stopped in one corner and gazed at Moore. "You could put bunk beds in here, you know, and bring your kids down."

The trooper gave a quick shake of his head.

"Why not?"

"Barb wanted custody. I didn't contest it. A cop's life is hell on a marriage."

"I s'pose."

Moore didn't respond. After some moments of silence, he led the way back out into the hall. "Bathroom down there," he said, waving a hand toward an open door.

Click drifted that way. He leaned in. "Would you look at that, an old claw-foot tub just like the one I've got."

"I'd prefer a shower, but the tub's it."

"In Nam, we'd tell each other stories on what we missed most about home. I said for me it was soaking in a tub. You get so hog dirty in a war." Click glanced back over his shoulder. "You in Nam?"

Moore pulled at the front of his T-shirt. "Germany. Army made me an MP. Shipped me to Krautland."

"Nice duty?"

"When you weren't cracking heads in the bars on Saturday nights, yeah."

"Kids get away from home, they want to raise a little hell."

"I guess."

A voice interrupted. "Are you two old duffers going to bore each other, or are you going to bring in the couch?"

At the end of the hall stood Garrison, her hands braced against her hips.

Moore saluted.

"Well, get to it."

"Yes ma'am. Right away, ma'am."

"Missus C and I've started lunch. You've got fifteen minutes."

"But I don't have any groceries."

"Scott, I know where the store is."

He raised his hands in surrender.

"Smart boy," Click whispered. "Never argue."

Again Garrison disappeared back into the kitchen.

Moore and Click went out onto the landing. They wrestled the shabby couch in through the doorway and set the couch against the long wall. Moore shimmed a leg with a magazine.

"Sad lookin' thing," Click said.

"It is, but I'll throw a blanket over it."

"Sure be an improvement."

Next they toted in the boards, three long ones—eight feet each—and two short ones.

They went back out for the bricks. Click studied the pile. "There is a way to get them inside faster than carrying them. You up for a game of catch?"

Moore rubbed his hands on his jeans. "I suppose you want to be the pitcher?"

"Well, it is my idea. Anyway, you know how many bricks you want in each stack before you put a board across. I don't."

Moore dashed inside. He slid up beside the boards and crouched for the first catch.

Click lofted a brick to him. Moore snatched it from the air and slapped it in place on the floor.

Two more bricks came flying. Moore snagged both. He set them a short distance to either side of the first brick, then positioned the first long board across them.

Click fired in another brick and another. He kept pitching until Moore had his stacks tall enough that he could position the second board.

Click brightened. "How about we pick up the pace?" he said and let fly with a barrage of bricks, Moore grabbing them, stacking them, his forehead slicking up from sweat.

A brick sailed past Moore. It banged off the wall, gouging the plaster.

"What are you two doing out there?"

Moore froze, as did Click.

"Nothing," Moore said.

The word came as an automatic reflex, of a boy caught doing something he knew he shouldn't.

He and Click waited for the worst.

When Garrison didn't come out, Moore relaxed, and Click, too. Click mopped his face with his shirt sleeve, then set about gathering up the last of the bricks. Moore scrambled after the errant one halfway across the room.

With that brick and Click's, he built out the bookcase and topped the unit with the short boards to either side, creating a well in the middle. Moore lifted his television into that space. He plugged the TV in and snapped the 'On' switch on. Static crackled through the cheap speaker in the television's plastic cabinet, and the black on the picture tube gave way to snow.

"If I want to see snow, I just look out the window," Click said.

Moore twiddled with the coat hanger. The swirling flakes let up, and 'The Days of Our Lives' came through. "Ahh, my favorite soap."

"You kidding?"

"Of course." Moore snapped the television off.

"Do you have the table set up?" Garrison asked from the bowels of the kitchen.

"Not yet."

"Well, get to it. We're bringing out the dogs."

"The what?"

"You'll see."

Click skated back out to the landing. There he yanked a card table from the clutter that had come up from the trailer. He flung the table through the doorway. Moore grabbed the table out of the air. He snapped the legs out and set the table down in front of the bay window.

Click slid up beside Moore, two folding chairs in each hand. "You can really move on this floor, you know that?"

The two did a 'ta-da' and held their hands out to the table and chairs just so as Garrison came in from the kitchen. She gave Moore and her father an indulgent smile as one would idiot children.

She carried a platter of buns and hot dogs from which rose vaporous steam. Missus C followed with a serving tray laden with bowls of chili, coleslaw, onions, sweet pickle relish, and the other stuff of lunch, including a bag of taco chips she clutched in her fingers curled beneath the tray. "I've got a pan of mint brownies in the kitchen I baked for you for dessert."

"And ice cream," Garrison said as she dealt out paper plates and napkins.

Missus C put her tray on the table, and Garrison waved for everyone to sit.

Click snatched off his cap. He stuffed it in his pocket before he pulled a chair out for Missus C. She sat down, and he took the chair to her right.

Garrison didn't wait for Moore to be a gentleman. She slipped into the chair to Missus C's left before he could reach for it.

Moore—the last standing—settled on the only vacant chair. It faced across the table to Missus C.

Click looked at Garrison. He pointed a finger up, then down. She nodded and said to Moore, "Take my hand."

"Why?"

"We're going to pray."

"I don't do that."

"You do today."

Click bowed his head.

The others followed his lead.

"Gracious God," he said, his voice hushed, "we thank You for food, for warmth, for roofs over our heads, for good friends and good family. You have blessed us so richly. We know, of course, that the richest blessing is the birth of Your Son, placed here to bring us to You. Help us to remember that that is the reason for this time, for this season. We ask now Your blessing on these simple foods, that they may keep us strong so we can do the chores at hand. We ask it, as always, in Jesus' name. And they all said—"

"Amen."

Click and Garrison spoke in unison, Missus C and Moore a half-beat behind.

Missus C patted Click's hand. "Thank you. It's been a long time since I've had a praying man in the house."

"You been alone now, what?"

"Almost twenty years. My Edwin died just before you went to Korea."

"He was a good man."

"The very best."

While Click and Missus C talked, Garrison laid a hot dog in her bun and scooped on chili and coleslaw. She skipped the onions and mustard for the pickle relish as the final topping. Garrison peered at Moore's hot dog, squinted at the almost invisible squirt of mustard on it. "That's it? You some kind of Yankee?"

Before he could answer, she set her hot dog down and ladled chili and slaw on his.

Moore, when she finished, stared at the conglomeration for the longest time. "You're strange."

"Get used to it."

****

Moore and Garrison stood in the doorway, surveying the great front room. It looked so much larger than it was because it had so little in it–a couch, the chair shaped like a hand, the brick-and-board bookcase half full with Moore's library, and the card table.

"You know, I really could put a grand piano in here," Moore said, "even a harp, a harpist, and a string quartet."

She bumped his hip.

He bumped back.

Both giggled like small children at play.

Garrison pulled on a waist-length jacket. "Come on, we better get a tree."

Moore got his sweatshirt and ball cap, and went to the bedroom for gloves. While he was gone, Garrison put on a hat of black fake fur that she had stowed in the sleeve of her jacket.

When he returned, he bent down to kiss her cheek, but thought better of it. They had worked together, off and on for the last months on the Wilson estate and the

Taylor murder, she the lawyer, he the investigator. They had shared a supper at the Sunshine Café. They had become friends, good friends, Moore thought. It was she who had put him on to this place.

At the top of the staircase, Garrison put her hand on the banister. "I dare you."

"What, to slide down that? You're nuts."

"Old fud." She got up on the banister, sidesaddle.

"You're going to do it."

"Of course."

"Hey, wait."

"For what?"

"At least let me get down to the bottom to catch you. You crash and break your leg, I got to explain that to your dad."

Garrison threw her hands up, but she waited while Moore clattered down the stairs. At the bottom, he made a production of bracing himself for the catch of this hundred-thirty-five-pound Tennessee beauty.

She shoved off, arms out, legs out, laughing as if she had no cares at all—down and off the end of the banister into his arms. Moore spun around and fell.

Missus Caudileski dashed into the hallway. "You all right?" she asked when she found Moore and Garrison in a jumble by her front door.

He gazed over Garrison lying across his chest. "Just sliding on the old banister."

"Children, children, children." Missus C took hold of Garrison's arm. She helped her up. "My boys were always doing that."

"Not me. Her," Moore said from the floor.

"Amanda, shame on you. You're a lady."

"So Pop keeps telling me." She straightened her hat before she reached down and helped Moore. "Missus C, haven't you ever slid down that banister?"

The corners of the woman's mouth curled into a smile. "Twice as I remember."

"We're going out to get a Christmas tree. You want to come along?"

"Oh, I already have mine up," she said. She opened the outside door for them. "You two have a good time."

They went out into the chill of the late afternoon, the sun gone, masked by a low deck of slate-gray clouds that had drifted in from the west, clouds that had drifted on beyond Morgantown until the higher reaches of Cullowhee Mountain blocked their passage further to the east. Given time, the clouds would slide up and over the mountain, but snow squalls would hide the movement from human eyes.

The two hunched up as they walked along, their gloved hands stuffed in their pockets. They made the turn at the end of the block and went on to a Christmas tree lot across the street from the Quick Mart. The operator, Holly Clifton, had already turned the lot lights on—a string of bare forty-watters—by the time Garrison and Moore arrived, their breaths crystalline in the air.

Clifton hurried out of the tiny trailer that served as his warming house and office. "Amanda, how you?" the tree seller called out. He pulled the earlappers of his plaid cap down over his earlobes.

"Just fine, Holly. We've come for a tree."

"Yer pap got one a couple weeks ago, didn't he?"

"Yes. This is for–" She tilted her head toward Moore.

Clifton's mittened hand came out. "Holly Clifton," he said.

Moore's gloved hand met Clifton's. "Scott Moore."

"You new here?"

"Guess you could say that. Just moved into the apartment at Missus Caudileski's."

"Oh, that's good. That's a fine place," the tree seller said. "And Missus Caudileski, they don't come no better. I sold her a tree last week."

To Garrison, Clifton fluffed out his beard. "Whatdaya think, Amanda, do I look like Santy Claus?"

"A skinny Santa Claus."

"I got to work more on my eatin'. Well, Mister Moore, let me show you the trees."

Clifton led off to the side of the trailer. He studied several trees before he plucked out one. "I only got about a dozen left. They been pretty well picked over, but this un's pretty good."

"Fir, isn't it?" Moore asked.

"Yup, Frasier fir, finest of Christmas trees." Clifton banged the stump on the ground several times. "See? No loose needles."

"How much?"

"Eight dollars."

Moore took off a glove to finger the bills in his pocket. He glanced at the tree and at Garrison, then the other trees, she studying him.

"Why don't we look at the other trees for a moment?" he said.

"Sure, you go right ahead."

Moore nudged Garrison down the line.

"What's the matter?" she whispered.

"I've only got four dollars left, and payday's not 'til the second."

She put a hand in her jacket pocket and pulled out a bill and some change. She counted. "I've got a dollar and thirty, thirty-five, thirty-seven cents. You're welcome to it."

"You're more broke than I am." He leaned a tree out of the line and gazed at it, put it back, and examined another. He put that one back, too, and pulled out a third.

Disapproval showed on Garrison's face. "It's got a bad side."

"Yes. Maybe he'll let it go cheap." Moore carried the tree over to Clifton, turning it so the tree seller was sure to see the misshapen side, a side that seemed to be missing half its branches. "How much?"

"Can't say I'm proud of that one. You got a corner you can maybe put that bad side in?"

"Maybe."

Clifton rubbed at his shoulder. "Tell you what, I'd take two bucks for it."

"Just a minute." Moore marched away, back down the line. He pulled out a second Scotch pine that could have been a sister to the first. He carried the tree back. "How much for the two of them?"

"You got two corners?"

"Maybe."

"Four dollars."

"Mister Clifton–"

"Call me Holly."

"Holly, these trees aren't likely to sell, are they?"

Clifton traced in the snow with the toe of his boot.

"You're going to have to throw them away after Christmas, aren't you?"

"No, I'll skin the branches off and cut 'em up for firewood."

"What do you say to three dollars for the both of them?"

Clifton continued his tracing. "Three-fifty."

"Three-ten."

"Three-forty."

"Three-twenty."

"Three-twenty, huh?"

"My best offer."

"How about three-thirty? I could maybe go down to three-thirty."

Moore spun the second tree around. "Split the difference."

Clifton glanced up from beneath his eyebrows, a smile exaggerating the crow's feet at the corners of his eyes. "Deal. You got tree stands?"

"Uh-huh." Moore pressed four bills into the tree man's mittened hand. Clifton shucked out three quarters and handed them back. The trooper then worked a hand into the middle of each tree and hefted the butt ends up over his shoulders. "Shall we go?" he said to Garrison.

They started away.

"Amanda?" Clifton called out.

She turned back.

The tree man traced in the snow again, a shy smile showing. "You got a pretty good businessman there."

"Oh, he's not mine."

"Maybe he should be. Speakin' of business, I'm not a young feller anymore. I'm thinkin' maybe I ought to be gettin' a will, maybe one for the missus, too. You bein' a lawyer an' all–"

"I can help you with that."

"That's good. Maybe you'd stop by the house one evening?"

"I'll talk to you tomorrow. We'll find a time."

"Well, you have a good Christmas, and you, too, Mister Moore."

"Scotty."

"Yessir, Scotty. And tell yer friends I still got a few trees left."

It was as if Clifton didn't want to let them go, and at that moment Garrison realized the old tree seller was lonely with so few customers in these last days before

Christmas. She wondered what he did in that trailer of his to pass the time. Was he a reader? She didn't know.

"Holly's never cut up a Christmas tree for firewood in his life," she said as she moved along beside Moore and the trees he carried on his shoulders.

"How's that?" he asked.

"Old Holly knows everybody who doesn't have a tree. Christmas Eve, he goes around town, leaving his unsolds on porches. He sets a tree beside a door, knocks, then runs off before anybody can answer."

"And they don't know?"

"Huh-uh."

"Then how do you know?"

"Pop and I saw him one year, when we were coming home from church."

They scuffled on, rounding the corner of the street that led to Missus Caudileski's. Garrison and Moore heard singing. As they got closer, they made out in the gloom of the late afternoon a cluster of people—adults and children—in Missus C's front yard, serenading her. *We three kings of Orient are, / bearing gifts we traverse afar—*

"Come on," Garrison said and bumped Moore into a trot.

Field and fountain, moor and mountain / following yonder star—

They cut through someone's front yard and dashed up beside the carolers.

*Oh-oo, star of wonder, star of night / star with royal beauty bright / westward leading, still proceeding / guide us to Thy perfect light—*Moore now boomed along with the carolers.

Several turned to the new voice but saw only greenery next to Garrison.

"Oh, come in, come in," Missus C called to the group, her face radiant. "I've got cookies."

The children stampeded for the porch and the front door, but the adults hung back. A number greeted Garrison, and she introduced Moore, he nodding and speaking from between the trees. The adults, members of the neighborhood Lutheran church, broke away in ones and twos to follow after their children.

Garrison and Moore also went in, only they diverted up the stairs where, at the top, they kicked off their shoes and went inside the flat.

Moore laid the trees down in front of the bay window. He strolled out into the hallway, to the bedroom closet, where he rummaged some and returned with an outsized tree stand in one hand and a toolbox in the other. "We're going to make us one tree," he said.

Garrison laughed.

"You doubt me, wench?"

"Well–"

"Pick up that tree." Moore motioned to the one closest to Garrison.

She hauled it up and held it steady, watching–fascinated–as he mated the other tree to it. Moore wove the branches of the two bad sides together until the tree trunks shouldered against one another.

"I got 'em now," he said, taking hold of the trees. "In my toolbox is some picture wire."

"So?"

"So cut me a couple lengths, and I'll tie these trunks together."

Garrison snipped two hanks of wire. She handed them to Moore, and he wrapped them around the trunks, both low and high. He then jammed the trunks into the tree stand. Moore hunkered down onto his belly and reached under the trees, for the bolts in the stand.

He turned them in—one, then the other, and the third—while Garrison held the twins straight.

"How's it look?" he asked as he twisted on the last bolt.

She stepped away, then strolled around the mended tree, measuring with her eye how the mated trees stood to vertical. "It's just amazing. Scott, it's amazing. Do you have any lights?"

"Barb got 'em, and I got the ratty tree stand. Some settlement."

A knock at the door interrupted.

"Would you see who that is?" Moore asked as he crawfished out from under the tree. He rolled up on his butt to admire his creation.

Garrison, at the door, opened it. There stood Missus Caudileski with a box wrapped in Christmas paper. "I saw your tree, or should I say trees? Could Mister Scotty use some lights? I got an extra string here."

"Scott?" Garrison asked.

He scrambled to his stockinged feet. "Lights? How did you know?"

"Well, you brought in two trees. I just guessed you might need some extra lights." Missus C peered at the tree in the bay window. "Oh, that's a pretty one. Where'd you put the other?"

"There is no other."

"Pardon?"

"That's it. I put them together."

She went closer and examined the mated trees. She poked around the ends of the branches. "Well, isn't that clever?"

Missus C gave the box to Moore. "You put the lights on, and I'll go down and get some cookies. And I've got the best hot rum punch. I made it for us, not the Lutherans."

She hurried away, out onto the landing and down the stairs.

Garrison swung quarter to Moore. She pursed her lips to restrain a laugh. "How is it having your own grandmother to look after you?"

"You think she'd mend my socks?"

"Don't you dare ask her to do that." She took the box from Moore. "I'll hold this, and you string the lights."

He peered inside. There on top laid something wrapped in tissue paper. Moore lifted it out. With the utmost care, he unwrapped the object and let the paper fall to the floor.

"It's a star," Garrison said.

"And it's got a light in it. Well, this goes on top." Moore went up on his toes. He reached the star high and settling it at the pinnacle of the twin trees. Then he dug into the box for the end of the string of lights. He found it and plugged the star into it. Moore then laid the lights—big Nomas normally reserved for outdoor trees—in among the branches. He and Garrison worked their way around and around the tree again. On the fifth circuit, out came the last of the lights and an extension cord. Moore plugged this into a wall socket.

On came the lights.

Blue lights.

Except for the star. It glowed a soft golden yellow.

Garrison, at the dimmer switch, turned the lights of the chandelier down, then out. She drifted to the center of the room and stood there, gazing at the tree, at the lights, at the star, mesmerized. This is Christmas, she thought. No tinsel, no fake snow, no beribboned boxes elbowing for space beneath the tree. Just sweet silence, the smell of pine, and a tree ever green—the assurance of life.

Moore came up beside her. He slipped his arm around her waist.

She looked up, her gaze meeting his. "Are you going to kiss me?" she asked.

"What?"

She pointed up, to a sprig of mistletoe that hung beneath the chandelier.

Bump and the Stranger

Bump Asher sat in his gas station on a frigid Christmas Eve afternoon. He hadn't been anywhere in years, not since his wife had died. He had no decorations at the house or here, no tree, no lights, nothing to add any cheer to either place. To the old garage man, this was just another day for work.

It wasn't that Bump hated Christmas. He didn't. It was just that without Dixie, his wife of a third of a century, he couldn't find a reason to celebrate. And they had had no children, so indeed he was alone.

He sat there on the edge of his smudged and oil-stained desk, the office redolent with the smell of gear grease and strong coffee. Bump gazed out through the plate-glass window at the snow that had been falling for the last hour, wondering if maybe he shouldn't turn the Open sign over and go home. But someone shuffled out of the gathering gloom and into the light of his gas pumps, a man with his hands stuffed deep in his pockets, his back hunched against the weather.

Kind of raggedy. Could he be one of those bums that had drifted down from Knoxville, one of those homeless fellows, as the preacher called them, living under the bridge at the other side of town? Could be.

The man came to the station door. He opened it and stepped inside, stamping the snow from the cracked leather of his shoes. "Mind if I warm myself for a minute, mister?"

"I was about to close," Bump said, not stirring from his seat on the edge of the desk, his arms folded across his chest. "There's a chair there by the space heater. Go ahead and sit a spell."

The stranger bobbed his head. He drifted over to the heater and held his hands out. He warmed them, rubbing them, massaging in the heat radiating from the kerosene burner.

There was something about the man's jacket. Faded and patched as it was, there on the back, Bump was sure of it, was a faint outline of South Vietnam and words stitches in a half-moon above it. What did they say? Thirty-Seventh Hellraisers, Tan-Wo? He hadn't seen a jacket like that in decades. "You in Nam?"

"That and a lot of other places," the stranger said.

"Army?"

The man shrugged, his longish hair, in need of a wash, dripping melting snow.

"Yeah, me, too," Bump said. "Long time ago. Where you livin'?"

"Here and there."

"Kinda understand." Asher picked up the large-mouth thermos from beside him. He screwed off the cap. "Friend, you look like you need a little something in your belly. Try this. Stew. Hot and tasty if I do say so myself. Made it this morning."

The stranger attempted a smile as he accepted the thermos, then sat and sipped at the thick broth.

"Easier with a spoon," Bump said. He leaned back and took a large spoon from the open center drawer of his desk. He tossed it to the man.

At that moment, the driveway bell dinged. Bump glanced up to see a 'Forty-Nine Ford coupe at his pumps, steam rolling out through the car's bullet-nosed grill. "My Lordy, would you look at that antique. Guess I better get out there and see what the driver wants."

At the door, he turned back. "When you're finished with that stew, you help yourself to some coffee on the hotplate. It's fresh."

Bump didn't wait for a response, but trotted out into the late afternoon, to the car, to the window open on the driver side. He leaned down. "You got troubles here?"

"Yes, mister, can you help me?"

Asher saw panic in the young man's face. What was that accent, Spanish? Mexican? Puerto Rican?

"My wife is about to have a baby. I got to get her to the hospital and my car's broken."

"Well, let me take a look. Pull the hood release." Bump pushed back from the door. He moved around to the front of the car and fitted the fingers of his mittened hand into the slot between the top of the grill and the hood. He felt for the paddle release that would pop the hood up, found it, and squeezed his fingers against the paddle until he heard a sproing. Then Bump lifted. He shoved the front of the hood up and out of the way. Steam billowed out, wreathing Bump's face and fogging his glasses and filling his nose with the stink of boiling coolant.

The garage man pulled a hanky from his back pocket. He dried his glasses and, after he got the bows hooked back over his ears, peered into the engine compartment. *Aww jeez, block must be cracked.*

Bump leaned around the hood. "Son, you ain't going anywhere in this thing."

"But mister—"

"Son, your car's dead." He turned away and went back to the station.

"But mister, I need help."

Bump didn't hear those last words. He went on inside, to a board that hung on the wall behind his desk, next to the AC Delco calendar. He took down the keys to his old Dodge truck, twenty years newer than the steaming car at the pumps, but still old. Bump moved on into the service bay where he kept his truck when he had no vehicles to work on. He ran up the overhead door, fired up the Dodge, and backed it out to where the young couple stood huddled next to their expired car.

"Take my truck," he said as he got out. "She ain't the best thing you ever looked at, but she'll get you to the hospital."

"I don't know, mister."

"It's this or walk. I don't think I can get a taxi out here."

"All right then. I got a little money."

"You keep it. You're gonna be needin' it."

"Well, thank you."

Bump shrugged. He turned to the young woman who, from her size, looked like she had all her possessions stuffed up under her coat. "Come on, missy," he said, "let me give you a hand," and he guided her around to the passenger side. Bump helped her step up and in while the husband pushed a suitcase in from the driver's side of the cab.

"You know where the hospital is now, don'tcha?"

The husband got in and yanked the driver's door shut. "Yes, mister," he said. "You're a savior."

"Aw, not really. You just drive careful. It's slick out there—and I'll call ahead to tell the hospital to expect you." He pushed the passenger door closed. Bump stepped back and watched the couple and the truck roll away out the drive, turn onto the street, and speed off.

"Well," he said to the spirits of the evening. He turned away, back to the service bay. Inside, Bump rolled the door down. He called to the stranger as he went on into the office, "Glad I loaned 'em the truck. Fella, you should see the tires on their car. They're shot, too."

But the stranger was gone. There on the desk stood the thermos—empty—and beside it a used styrofoam coffee cup.

The garage man rubbed at the short gray hair on the back of his neck. *Well, at least he got something in his belly.*

Finding himself with nothing to do and no one to talk to, Bump Asher went back outside, figuring he might see whether the wreck of a Ford would start. The driver had left the key in the ignition. Bump twisted the key and held it as the engine cranked. He pumped on the accelerator, squirting more gasoline into the carburetor. That wealth of gas shot into each cylinder on successive downstrokes and ignited, and the engine roared to life.

Bump listened to the engine as he continued pumping on the accelerator. He shifted the transmission into first gear, eased out the clutch, and car rolled away from the pumps. Bump guided the coupe into the open service bay where he stopped it and turned off the motor.

The old girl ain't so dead after all.

He slipped out from behind the steering wheel. Bump took down a trouble light and leaned across the fender to inspect the driver's side of the engine. If the block was indeed cracked—

But no water leaked from there, nor from the right side of the motor—the passenger's side.

Bump Asher used the hook at the end of the trouble light as a scratcher. He worked it over a sideburn as he moved around front, and that's when he saw it, water puddling beneath the radiator. The garage man got down on one knee. He peered more closely. There was a drip there, a pretty good drip. He reached up underneath for the hose coming out at the bottom of the radiator. His fingers felt the hose all right, spongy and wet.

Shoot. Ahh well, at least it's an easy fix.

The garage man pushed back up. He rubbed at his knee. Arthritis and a cold concrete floor, not a good combination. Bump forced his knee to work as he went over to a wall where an assortment of hoses and V-belts hung. He hummed as he looked them over and took one hose down. *Yeah, that's the right one.*

Asher drained the radiator. When he had that done, he changed out the old, rotted radiator hose for the new one. Not a bad job. Bump flushed the radiator and refilled it with new coolant. He studied the new hose, saw that it held. Not a drop leaked out from anywhere.

Next he examined the car's tires, ran a hand over the tread of the first, then the next and the next, all as bald as a baby's bottom Bump's father would have said. *These sure aren't gonna get 'em through the winter.*

To the side, in the next bay, resided Dixie Asher's old Lincoln, the model with the suicide doors, the sucker longer than Bump's pickup. He kept the Lincoln parked there, tires like new. He didn't need the car, only drove it enough to keep the battery up, but Bump just couldn't part with the old boat because Dixie had loved it so.

So he ran the Lincoln up on the hoist, and the Ford, too, each enough that he could hit their wheels' stud bolts with an air wrench without having to bend over, and he went about swapping the wheels and tires from one car to the other. Bump hadn't quite finished when he heard what sounded for certain like a backfire. He leaned into the office, to peer out through the plate-glass window. A county cruiser idled by his pumps and–

The air wrench dropped from Bump's hand. He bolted for the office door, yanked it open, and ran outside to a deputy lying by the cruiser, the snow crimson at the man's shoulder.

"Charlie?" Bump called out as he went down on his knees beside the officer, the officer hatless.

Charlie Debbs coughed against the cold and the pain. "Bump?" he whispered.

"Yeah. Gawddamn, what the hell happened to you?"

"Shot . . . gotta help me."

"That's for damn sure." Asher got one arm under Debbs' knees and the other under the deputy's shoulders. He lifted and pushed up with his legs, his arthritic knee almost buckling under the strain. But it held and Bump shuffled with his burden through the snow toward the office. Turning, he backed through the doorway, using his butt to keep the door open. Inside, he turned again and lowered Debbs onto a ragged overstuffed chair he kept for people who waited while he worked on their cars and pickups.

"Blood's gonna get all over," the deputy wheezed.

"Maybe, but who's to notice?"

Bump's mind raced back over the medic training he'd received all those decades ago. *Pressure, pressure, yeah, that's it. That stops the bleeding.*

The laundry company that serviced his station had been there that morning, and the route man had left a stack of clean shop towels. Bump ran out into the service bay. He grabbed up a handful and a roll of duct tape, and ran back. Bump tore the shoulder of Debbs' uniform jacket open, the jacket reeking of cigarette smoke. He ripped away the shoulder of the shirt as well, to get at the wound. With the shop cloths and the tape, Bump bound the wound, smiling at Debbs as he worked. "They say duct tape can fix anything. You hurtin', buddy?"

"Yeah."

"Think I got something." From his jacket pocket, Bump produced a bottle of pain pills the doctor had given him for his back.

"These'll do ya," he said as he shook a half-dozen into Debbs' hand. Bump got a cup of water and held it to the deputy's lips as Debbs swallowed pill after pill. "Hard work I know, but you hang in there. I'll getcha an ambulance out here."

Telephone . . . call . . . Bump slapped the side of his face. "I was supposed to call the hospital."

He fumbled with the receiver. When he got it to his ear, he heard nothing—no dial tone. "Charlie, line must be out. S'pose I could get one of your buddies on the radio in your car?"

Debbs coughed hard, creating for himself a new wave of pain. He winced and clutched at his shoulder. "You'll get the dispatcher."

"Who's on tonight?"

"Gracie."

"Then we're home safe." Bump trooped outside only to find that a bullet had gone into the cruiser's dashboard, destroying the police radio. He trudged back. "Charlie boy, we're in a helluva fix. Your radio's gone."

"Maybe I can drive," Debbs said. He coughed again, his head racheting forward with the force of it, as he tried to get up. He fell back into the chair, and Bump held him down.

The deputy wheezed, his hand going to his shoulder. "Guess I'm not going anywhere, am I? Thanks for not leaving me out there."

"Hey, buddy boy, what are friends for?"

"Guy that shot me, he's still got to be around. He's on foot."

"That's as may be, but I tell ya, he's the least of our worries." Bump dragged over one of his folding chairs and sat in front of Debbs. There he peeled back the bandage, lifting his head so he could squint through the bottom part of his tri-focals. "Bleeding's pretty well stopped, Charlie boy."

Bump prodded at the wound. "Looks a helluva lot worse than it is. Bullet passed right through the fat of your shoulder. If it hit any bone, it only nicked it. Can't feel anything shattered. Charlie, old buddy, if I was a bettin' man, I'd bet your pay you're gonna be all right in a month or two. Whatdaya say to a cup of my coffee?"

Debbs shook his head.

"Best in town and you know it. Too bad I don't have any donuts."

The deputy laughed. He twisted, his face creased with pain. "Always the donut jokes. You know I'm diabetic."

"Yeah, I do."

The outside door burst open. In ran a wild-eyed youth in faded jeans and a denim jacket, waving a pistol. "Gimme your cash! I gotta have your cash!"

Bump twisted around to the kid. He saw the boy's hand shaking. "Whoa there, fella. I don't want you shootin' out any of my glass, and I sure don't want you shootin' me."

"Come on, money!"

The deputy touched Bump's hand. "He's the one."

"I figured."

The kid turned more toward the wounded Debbs, but before the kid could do anything, Bump came out of his chair. He stood between the two. "Son, you need to put that cannon away. I got money in my pocket, so you back off a bit."

"Want the money from your cash register, too." The boy waved his pistol at the ancient manual NCR machine on Bump Asher's desk, the back of the cash register papered over with business cards anyone who came through Bump's station always left.

"Oh, I'm sorry about that," the garage man said.

"Why?"

"I already made my bank deposit for the day. All you're gonna get is my walking-around money."

"How much?"

Bump's hand went into the pocket of his blue twill trousers. When his hand came out, it held three bills– two twenties and a five. Bump heard the deputy move behind him. He glanced back and saw Debbs' hand go toward his holster and the Glock it contained. The garage man reached back. "Charlie, you leave that. We already got one gun too many out as it is."

Bump turned his focus on the young man. "Son, it's Christmas Eve. You take the money. Just put that pistol away."

He held out the bills. As Bump gave them over, he also reached for the barrel of the gun. He got hold of it. The kid, his eyes tearing up, released his grip on the weapon and fell to his knees, sobbing.

Bump gazed at the kid. "Not too good at being a bad man, are ya?"

"All I wanted was to buy something for my wife and little boy," the kid blubbered between sobs. "Lost my job, my car. Behind on the damn rent."

Bump passed the gun, a Smith & Wesson, to Debbs. "Son, we all get in a bit of squeeze now and then. Take it from an old man who's been there, but we make it through the best we can."

He reached down. Bump caught the kid by the arm and helped him up into a chair. He filled a clean styrofoam cup with coffee. "You know," he said, pressing the cup in the kid's hand, "sometimes we do stupid things. Being stupid, that's what makes us human, and you comin' in here with a gun, let me tell you that was stupid. Suppose we see if we can get this thing sorted out."

The young man mopped at his tears and rubbed the sleeve of his jacket at his dripping nose. He glanced over at the deputy. "I'm sorry. I'm sorry I shot you."

"Oh, shut up and drink your damn coffee."

Bump twisted toward Debbs, his eyes wide in surprise.

****

Sirens came wailing up the street, two of them. A city police cruiser swung into the gas station and a box on wheels–an ambulance–right behind it, both skidding in the snow. A patrolman bailed out of the cruiser. He came on the run, gun drawn, through the station's door.

"Charlie, you all right?" he called to Debbs.

"Yeah, but I've had better days. . . . How'd you find me?"

"GPS locator went off in your car. When your dispatcher couldn't raise you, she called me to get out here. What happened?"

"Got shot."

The patrolman, Diz Walker–short and wiry–moved toward the kid, the only one in the gas station office he didn't know. "He the one who did this?"

"Naw. Guy ran off in the dark."

Bump and the young man glanced at one another.

"Dropped his gun, though," Debbs said. He held the kid's weapon out, butt first.

"Gawd, Charlie, you handle this, did ya?" Walker asked. "We won't be able to get any prints off it."

"Well, I wasn't thinking too clear."

Two paramedics pushed in. Bump knew them, Alice Goodhue and Jeff McKnight. He motioned them toward Debbs, and they, without exchanging so much as a word, went to work cleaning and rebandaging the deputy's wound.

Walker waved his pistol at the kid. "Who's this guy?"

"Works here," Debbs said.

Bump grinned. "Hired him this morning. Fella lost his job, and I'm gettin' a little too old to be working as a mechanic."

The patrolman holstered his pistol, a Glock like the deputy's. "Hell you say. Bump, you'll never quit. Who's gonna take care of my car if you do?"

"The kid here."

Finished, Goodhue and McKnight helped Debbs up. They moved him toward the door and their ambulance, all the lights still flashing. The young man reached out for Debbs' coat sleeve as the deputy went by. "Why?" he whispered.

Debbs stared at him. "It's Christmas," he said.

****

Some several minutes later, the ambulance pulled away and the city cruiser behind it. Bump Asher put a hand on the young man's shoulder. "Son, looks like you got one doozy of a break tonight. That ought to solve some of your problems, and I think maybe I can help you with one or two others."

He went into the back room and rummaged around the storage shelves. When he returned, he carried a cardboard box a bit larger than a whiskey case. Bump pawed inside it until he turned up what he was looking for—a ring box that fit in the palm of one's hand.

"Here you go," he said. "Something for your wife. I don't think my Dixie would mind. She told me the day she was dying that someday it would come in handy."

The young man took the ring box. With unsteady fingers, he opened it to see a modest gold band set with a crystal clear stone. "A diamond?"

"It isn't very big. Didn't have much money back when we got married."

"I can't take this. It means something to you."

Bump pushed the ring box back when the young man tried to return it. "Now it means something to you. I got my memories. That's enough."

He again reached into the big box. This time Bump brought out a Texaco tanker truck. "You say you got a boy, huh?"

"Yeah, five years old."

"Seems I remember boys like trucks. The oil company gave me a bunch of these last year to sell. Last one. Take it for your boy."

Tears again filled the young man's eyes. He mopped at them, then held out Bump Asher's folding money. "I can't take this."

"Now I'd like to know why the hell not? What are you gonna buy Christmas dinner with? Just count it as part of your first week's pay."

"You really giving me a job?"

"Didn't you hear me tell old Diz I need a mechanic?"

"Really?"

"Really. You know what a wrench is and a sparkplug, don't you?"

"Yeah."

"That's enough for a start. You better get on home to your family."

The kid rose. He moved toward the door, but turned back. "I'll be here in the morning—for work."

"Make it the day after. I don't open on Christmas."

Bump watched the door close and, through his station's plate-glass window, he watched the kid hustle away into falling snow and the darkening night, the rear end of the toy tanker truck sticking out from beneath his arm. When Bump turned back, the stranger was sitting at his desk. "Where'd you come from? I thought you left."

"I've been here. I've always been here." The corners of the stranger's mouth drew up in a smile.

"Man, I sure didn't see you."

"Bump—you don't mind if I call you Bump, do you?"

"That's kinda my name. I tell ya, fella, I'm gonna sit down. I'm pooped. It's been a gawd-awful long day."

The stranger stood. He waved Bump to the chair. "You say you don't celebrate Christmas. Why is that?"

Comfortable at last, Bump filled a chipped china mug with coffee, the mug emblazoned with a Crescent wrench and the slogan, 'World's greatest mechanic.' After he stopped pouring, he held the pot over the cup the stranger had used.

"No, thanks. What you gave me before was plenty."

The old garage man set the pot back on the hotplate. "Christmas?" he asked. "Well, after my Dixie died, I just couldn't see what all the bother was worth. Puttin' up a tree, baking cookies like I used to with Dixie. Just wasn't the same by myself."

Asher shook some sugar into his coffee. He stirred the brew with a pencil.

The stranger touched the garage man's shoulder. "Bump, what you do is Christmas. You gave me something to eat and drink when I was hungry, and warmed me when I was cold. That pregnant woman on the way to the hospital, you remember her?"

"Sure."

"She's already given birth to a son who will grow up to be a physician, a healer."

Bump smiled at that.

"The deputy you helped, your friend? A day's coming when he will save the lives of a dozen people who would otherwise die in a bridge washout. And that young man who tried to rob you, years after you're gone he will become a wealthy man, and he will share that wealth with tens of thousands of people. All this is the spirit of the season, Bump, and you keep it as good as any man."

The garage man arched an eyebrow. He glanced up, to better study the face of this person who stood beside him. "You sure you haven't been nippin' at a bottle of Jim Beam?"

The stranger shook his head.

"So how do you know all this, if you don't mind me asking?"

"Let's just say I got an inside track on this sort of thing." The stranger started toward the door, but he too, like the young man before him, turned back. "I should tell you one more thing."

Bump took his pencil from his coffee. He sucked the drops off.

"There will come a time, my friend, and it's not far off, you're going to see your Dixie. You're going to be with her." The stranger backed away toward the door. "I'd like to stay longer, but I can't."

The garage man sipped from his mug. "Why's that?" he asked.

"I have to be getting home. My father's planned a big celebration."

"Oh?"

"You see, tomorrow's my birthday."

"Well, um, happy birthday then."

The stranger left. Bump, as he rubbed a finger around the rim of his mug, watched the man in the faded Vietnam war jacket disappear into the snow and the night. He glanced down at his coffee, then back up. *Was there a radiance about him?*

About the author

Jerry Peterson has been writing stories ever since his parents gave him a toy rotary press for Christmas when he was 12. The next day, he set one of his kid stories in rubber type, inked up the press and ran it off . . . making Peterson a published author well before he was 13. Since then, he's written a mountain of news and feature stories for newspapers in Colorado, West Virginia, and Virginia. His short stories have appeared in several anthologies and now he has five novels in print, both as real books and e-books. Today, he lives and writes in his home state of Wisconsin, the land of dairy cows, craft beer, and good books.

Upcoming titles

Coming soon, *The Last Good Man*, the first book in a series of Wings Over the Mountains novels.

That will be followed by *Capitol Crimes*, the second book in this series . . . a mystery.

Made in the USA
Columbia, SC
23 March 2018